Twice Upon a Time

By Daniel Stern

NOVELS

The Girl With The Glass Heart

The Guests of Fame

Miss America

Who Shall Live, Who Shall Die

After The War

The Suicide Academy

The Rose Rabbi

Final Cut

An Urban Affair

SHORT STORIES

Twice Told Tales

Twice Upon A Time

19.95

Twice Upon a Time

S t o r i e s

Daniel Stern

W · W · Norton & Company

New York   London

Lines of poetry throughout this book are attributed as follows, and reprinted by kind permission:

"Never Give All the Heart" by W. B. Yeats, from *The Poems of W. B. Yeats: A New Edition*, edited by Richard J. Finneran (New York: Macmillan, 1983).

"Hugh Selwyn Mauberly" from *Personae* by Ezra Pound. Copyright © 1926 by Ezra Pound. Reprinted by permission of New Directions Publishing Corp.

"What my lips have kissed, and where, and why" by Edna St. Vincent Millay. From *Collected Poems*, Harper & Row. Copyright © 1923, 1951 by Edna St. Vincent Millay and Norma Millay Ellis. Reprinted by permission of Elizabeth Barnett, literary executor.

The Complete Poems of Emily Dickinson, edited by Thomas H. Johnson, copyright © 1935 by Martha Dickinson Bianchi; copyright © renewed 1963 by Mary L. Hampson, by permission of Little, Brown and Company.

The Collected Poems of Wallace Stevens by Wallace Stevens, copyright © 1954 by Wallace Stevens. Reprinted by permission of Alfred A. Knopf, Inc.

Copyright © 1992 by Daniel Stern
All rights reserved
Printed in the United States of America
The text of this book is composed in 11/15 Linotype Walbaum
with the display set in Onyx
Composition and manufacturing by The Maple-Vail
Book Manufacturing Group.
Book and Ornament design by Margaret M. Wagner

Library of Congress Cataloging-in-Publication Data
Stern, Daniel
Twice upon a time / Daniel Stern
p. cm.
I. Title.
PS3569.T3887T884 1992
813'.54—dc20 92-11865
ISBN 0-393-03402-X
W.W. Norton & Company, Inc. 500 Fifth Avenue, New York, N.Y. 10110
W.W. Norton & Company Ltd., 10 Coptic Street, London WCIA 1PU
1 2 3 4 5 6 7 8 9 0

For Gloria

For the feast of heart and mind—
much gratitude and all love.

Contents

Author's Note

THE idea of putting a text by a previous writer at the *heart* of a piece of short fiction came to me one winter's day, while thinking about youth and its dreams. As I mulled over the elements of a story that was forming in my imagination—a beautiful, ambitious young woman, a cautious young man at a moment of choice, and a book, *The Liberal Imagination* by Lionel Trilling—I suddenly realized that I was as moved by recalling the experience of reading that book when I was a young writer as I was by any other element of my half-shaped story.

If the crucial element had been the beautiful young woman, surely I would not have hesitated to build the tale around her; theme, style, character, title and all. Well, I thought, why not place the Trilling text at the very center of the characters' experience? And why not call the story by the name of the book that had been so important to me? That way, my story would have a mirror-image behind it and the entire world of the imagination before it. It took a small leap of nerve, not to mention faith, but what got my pulses racing was this idea: that a text by a writer of the past whom I loved, even a non-fiction work, could be basic to a fiction; as basic as a love affair, a trauma, a house, a mother, a landscape, a lover, a job, or a sexual passion. Literature might actually make its claim; not merely as a subcategory of entertainment, education or culture, but as a branch of the fullness of life in the act of being lived.

"The Liberal Imagination by Lionel Trilling: a Story," became the first of a series of Twice Told Tales, a title borrowed, immodestly, from Hawthorne. My next sortie was a story based on the uncanny reaction I'd had the first time I came across Freud's *The Interpretation of Dreams*. This gradually became the comedy of a man who kept marrying widows, yet the basic ideas in Freud's essay carried the characters into the story, the way, in more innocent times, a bridegroom used to carry a bride across the threshold.

All this carried me across a threshold into a new house of fiction. I then tackled a new piece based on a short story. I chose, of all writers, Hemingway. The master. (The trick in these matters, as in all high wire acts, is not to look down and to keep your balance.) I wrote "A Clean, Well-Lighted Place by Ernest Hemingway: a Story."

Trickier, now, as you can see, because, unlike the Trilling nonfiction work or the Freud, this one already *was* a story. It was, in important ways, a story about a "place." And my story became a story about people without a true "place." Hemingway gave us two waiters in a cafe, one troubled, one matter-of-fact. I chose two men in the international motion picture world, one troubled and one a naïf; the former a man haunted by the Hemingway story. (There's no reason why a character can't be as passionate about a text as the author.)

These and several others made up the first volume in this new fictional experiment. It was called *Twice Told Tales.* But even before that book was published, more of these texts were "choosing" me; texts from which I needed to weave new stories. These were as varied as "Bartleby the Scrivener by Herman Melville," a story that has mystified generations and to which I have added my own mystifications; "A Hunger Artist by Franz Kafka," another famous puzzler; and "The Communist Manifesto by Karl Marx and Friedrich Engels," perhaps just to show that you could use just about *any* text to enrich and inform a new piece of fiction. And, as if to stretch that notion even further, I used poems by Wallace Stevens as keystones for two different stories. These, plus one other story by Hawthorne—one of *his* "twice told tales"—made up the book in hand, *Twice Upon A Time.*

These stories began to appear in magazines and while it was, as always, exciting to see a new one actually in print, the experience was not without its comic side.

Me: (to friend) Have you read "Wakefield by Nathaniel Hawthorne?"
Friend: Yes, it's an amazing story.
Me: Oh, thanks.
Friend: No, no, I haven't read *your* Hawthorne—I thought you meant . . . Hawthorne . . .

Well, you get the idea.

The writing of Twice Told stories made me another gift: it freed me from the constrictions of the typical narrator, who can all too easily be identified with the author. Somehow, by using the dramatic or comic essence drawn from an earlier writer, a distance is evoked and a liberation from the self takes place. A glance around any bookstore shows that it's all too easy, whether writing in the first or third person, to make a protagonist who is actually the author or the author's opinions and experiences, in an imperfect, Inspector Clouseau-like disguise. But the further I got from the "personal" voice, the more strongly I could deal with deeply personal material. This newfound dialogue with my well-loved, dead authors, enabled me to write, for example, about my dead father without using myself as the protagonist/antagonist. I cannot be too grateful for that gift.

As I tended these second growth literary vines, I found, too, that you didn't always need to make use of *every* theme, idea, category, or philosophical tendency of the original. After all, if you are writing a story about a student being expelled from school or about a painful divorce, you select only the events and emotions which make sense for your story. Thus in my "Aspects of the Novel by E. M. Forster" story, I confine myself almost completely to Forster's notion of what makes "flat" or "round" characters in fiction—and by extension, in life. On the other hand, in "The Communist Manifesto by Karl Marx and Friedrich Engels" I use a barrage of varied Marxist notions which obsess my characters, as engines to drive a picaresque story.

I'd assumed that this new game of exploration, invention, and rediscovery was my own private adventure. Until one day, students from a midwest university wrote me to say they were using *Twice Told Tales* as a model in their creative writing class. In due time along came a story by a young woman: "A Clean, Well-Lighted Place by Ernest Hemingway." (Certainly the first time in history that a woman has written a Hemingway story.) It was quite different from Hemingway's story or mine—but faithful in spirit. She chose to emphasize the element of light (as in "well-lighted"). The dramatic point was the issue of leaving the light on or turning it off, while making love. But the subtext was still the safety and order of light against the panic of darkness. The tale worked nicely. I felt like a father; or was it a grandfather?

Now, when I teach creative writing, I can point my students to a part of their lives they may never have thought of as a resource for their fiction: any piece of writing they've ever loved. When young, we all have encounters which leave us with significant memories. A boy, a girl, a teacher, a friend, a grandparent, whose special intensity, passionate or comic, touches us and leaves a permanent mark. Why not include in this company Tolstoy, Flaubert, Joyce, Fitzgerald, Henry James, Virginia Woolf, Ralph Ellison . . . Daisy Miller, Lambert Strether, Mrs. Dalloway, Jay Gatsby?

This is my partial list, make your own. Simply because these authors and characters appear only by way of small marks printed on a sequence of pages, and not in the flesh, does that make them less important to your mind and your spirit?

Some years ago I asked the writer Anaïs Nin, "Do you like Jorge Luis Borges?" She replied, "Well, yes, he's wonderful. [Pause] But he does smell of the *library*."

She was right, of course. Except that, along with the aroma of roses, early-morning fresh coffee and beach sand after the rain, the smell of the library is one of the blessings of the world. And those library shelves are filled with books silently waiting with the special patience of literature. Perhaps, as they are discovered and loved by new, young writers, they may become the soil from which fresh stories of the future may grow, enriched by the ideas, passions, and poetics of the past.

—Daniel Stern
New York, 1992

Acknowledgments

THE STORIES in this collection first appeared in the following publications:

Columbia: A Magazine of Poetry and Prose, "The Man With the Blue Guitar by Wallace Stevens"

Hayden's Ferry Review, "Sunday Morning by Wallace Stevens"

The Icarus Review, "Bartleby the Scrivener by Herman Melville"

Paris Review, "The Communist Manifesto by Karl Marx and Friedrich Engels," "A Hunger Artist by Franz Kafka"

Raritan: A Quarterly Review, "Wakefield by Nathaniel Hawthorne"

A Hunger Artist
by Franz Kafka

(a Story by Daniel Stern)

We don't have time enough to be ourselves. All
we have time for is to be happy. —*Camus*

We don't have time enough to be ourselves or
to be happy. All we have time enough for is our
work. And not enough for that. That's what
counts! —*Brandauer*

BRANDAUER had Tuna Fish for lunch every day of the nine years I knew him. Sometimes on rye toast, sometimes on white bread, sometimes with a Coke, sometimes with a small glass of milk. Not a full-size glass: the half sizes kids drink from. It took him about twelve minutes and he was ready to go back to work.

We met the year my second book was published—the one written with vanishing ink. I was also working as a rep for a production company which specialized in the fancy avant-garde commercials which were then in style. That was the year applause began to come to Brandauer, late and sudden. When it grew to a crescendo a few years later, while nothing much was happening in what we laughingly called my literary career, he felt a statement was called for. "Don't get too excited," he said. "And don't envy me. Coming at this time in my life, these honors are like rocks falling on my head." He was fifty-six, tall and lean as a panther. A grizzled Jewish Panther of the writing jungle. I didn't believe his disclaimer then, nobody did. Later it was another matter.

This late-bloomed success was the main reason we met. Brandauer had come out of his cage for a time. This never-photographed, never-interviewed, slowly famous, invisible comic artist of rigor and denial had actually agreed to teach a course at a creative writing workshop. And, as if one wonder were not enough, he also agreed to be interviewed.

The setting for these extraordinary events was to be a

small but serious writers' conference, near Seattle. Having been tapped by the *Paris Review* to do his long-refused interview, I sat in on his class. The fortunate few were early, notebooks out, necks craned upwards—Brandauer was six feet tall and thin and looked a little like Abraham Lincoln if Abraham Lincoln had been of Eastern European Jewish descent.

Everyone sitting around the long oval table waited, watching this man who had emerged from a dozen years at hard labor in solitary confinement, five in the Sheepshead Bay section of Brooklyn and seven in Genoa, Italy, learning, as one critic wrote, to make sentences walk, dance, and sing. There were three well-documented years in France, as well, where he'd lived in a stone house on a hill in a tiny perched village near Avignon. But there too he had mostly stayed in his stone room, performing his self-appointed task as the ballet master of the modern English sentence.

That's right—no wife, no children, all sorts of friends, but no family who could claim time away from his mission. Or so everyone thought at the time. Given this well-publicized first surfacing, the class's expectation was naturally high. If Brandauer knew this, he wasn't letting on. He picked up the small, green-covered book of stories by Kafka and began to read: *"A Hunger Artist. A story by Franz Kafka. During these last decades the interest in professional fasting has markedly diminished. . . . It used to pay very well to stage such great performances under one's own management, but today that is quite impossible. We live in a different world now."* In a short time it became terribly and comically clear that all Brandauer would teach, in what was advertised as his Creative Writing class, was one fourteen-page story by Kafka. No student self-expression, no handing in of manuscripts to be criticized by the classmates, no memorialized encouraging comments scribbled in the margins by the Master.

What he did give to the students was an eloquent over-view of a story about a man whose art was fasting; who practiced it in a cage, setting world records for taking little food sometimes, no food other times, for days, weeks, and finally many years—on his own and later in a circus. For a time, since the art of fasting itself had a large audi-ence, he was famous, successful—even as his ribs stuck through his skin. Later, the art falls out of fashion and the hunger artist dies, by now utterly forgotten. Into his cage they put a young panther; they bring him the food he likes . . . *"and the joy of life streamed with such ardent passion from his throat . . ."*

The kids were stunned. When Brandauer read the end in which the dying Hunger Artist whispers to the Over-seer that the audience should not admire his fasting— *"Because I have to fast, I can't help it"*—and explains, finally, *"Because,"* and here Brandauer hunched down and spoke the Artist's last words in a hoarse whisper, *"I couldn't find the food I liked. If I had found it, believe me, I should have made no fuss and stuffed myself like you or anyone else."*

He was a smash. The young people all around me were applauding, thrilled. They had clearly forgotten, in the excitement of the moment, that Brandauer had not even read a story of his own, let alone one of theirs; had not told them how they should write or even how he wrote, himself, except by inference. It was a subtle, allusive, brilliant performance. Several faculty members had invited themselves in, stood in the back, and they were going wild, too. The single exception was the striking young woman who sat next to me, shoving impatient hands through her long red hair. She never took her eyes off Brandauer. Either she was extraordinarily fair or her exquisite face was pale with some emotion I couldn't figure out. Actually, she looked the way people in books might look when "pale with anger."

While she stared at him and I stared at her, Brandauer made it clear but not pleasant to the students that *all* he would deal with was the way the story was made. No fancy hermeneutics; just how something is made.

"Look how Kafka has the audience *itself* take an active part in the Hunger Artist's dramatic fasting presentation. There are casual onlookers in front of his cage, but there are also *relays of permanent watchers selected by the public—usually butchers*, Kafka tells us—and they are to watch to make sure the Artist doesn't have some resource to secret nourishment. With two words, *usually butchers,* Kafka introduces humor into this grim business."

"Critics," one student called out.

Brandauer paused; he patted a pencil against the wire frame of his eyeglasses. He did not look at the waiting student. He smiled, as at a private joke. Then he proceeded: "Later, however," he said, "just before the end, not only is he not being scrutinized, but no one even notices the starving Hunger Artist; he's hidden beneath layers of straw, until an Overseer notices what seems to be an empty cage and pokes around until he discovers

the artist almost dead from his fast." So much for interpretations and analogies.

Brandauer must have sensed the restlessness, almost
a confusion in the air. "This is the way we will work,
here," he said, bending over the table on which lay the
book. Tall and skinny, he arched his back, one half of a
pair of parentheses, and explained that the only way he
knew to learn to write was to read. So, in the remaining
sessions they would read and reread and reread again
this small story by Kafka. "We will reinvent this strange
little story by one of the strangest writers who ever lived—
and then you'll go on to invent your own, that's what
counts. I'm sorry if you expected more or different. I can't
give more or different. This is the only way I know." It
was the first time I heard that phrase from him—"that's
what counts." It was not the last.

Outside, on the slippery steps of the conference hall,
Brandauer and I made arrangements to meet for the
interview. The inevitable Seattle drizzle huddled us under
umbrellas. I scribbled his address.

"Come at four. We'll do two hours, then I've invited
some people for dinner."

"I'll bring the wine."

"Don't bring anything. I have a bottle."

Suddenly there was a presence between our two
umbrellas. The young girl with the angry gaze, my class-
room neighbor, stood there. She had forgotten her
umbrella.

"Professor Brandauer . . ." she said.

"*Mister*," he said. "I don't profess anything. I'm just a
writer."

She pushed a bundle of manuscripts towards him. It was dauntingly large enough to be secured by a fat rubber band. Water streamed down her forehead past large, blue, unblinking eyes. I couldn't help thinking she looked like a water nymph in some Bernini Fountain in Rome; a beauty.

"Can I lend you my umbrella?" Brandauer said, an old-fashioned gentleman. He was carefully not looking at the papers she held.

"No," she said. "You can read my stories."

"They're going to be soaking wet." He moved to bring her into the protected circle, but she moved away, impatient.

"I came up from Newport News . . ." She paused as if searching for the strongest argument she could make. Indeed, I would have guessed even further south than Virginia, going by the music below the rage in the words.

". . . just to get your comments on my stories."

"You heard what I . . ."

"This-is-my-life, Mister Brandauer," she said. "I have read everything you've—"

"Only four books," he murmured. But anger had made her deaf to Brandauers's mild irony.

". . . and I didn't come all this soaking way to hear what's-his-name. I came to hear what you think about my—my—" I was afraid she was going to say her life, again; I'd seen Brandauer sort of wince the first time.

"What's *your* name?" Brandauer said.

"Penelope Anne Golden. You *will* read me, then."

I was impressed by the "read me." She couldn't have

been more than twenty-four and she already felt there
was a "me" to read.

"It wouldn't be f-f-f-fair to the others. T-t-t-hat's what
counts."

It was the first time I'd heard him stammer. He owned
one, but like the rest of his provenance, he used it spar-
ingly.

"I don't give a damn about the others," Penelope Anne
Golden said. "I came here for you!" She licked the rain
from her lips while her stone glance stayed on Brandauer's face.

"Miss Golden, you don't understand . . ."

"I don't have to," she said, and backing off a little, threw
the rubber-band-bound sheaf of papers at Brandauer. She
threw it underhand, a softball throw, and Brandauer had
to drop his umbrella to catch it. He stood there, like a
statue of himself, Penelope Anne Golden's life in his
hands, rain blinding his eyeglasses.

What I remember most about that first evening at the
tiny apartment Brandauer had rented in downtown Seattle was how lavishly we three dinner guests poured out
conversation, laughter, and information. It turned out none
of us had met before. The other two were two professors
of American Studies—married to each other and to
Brandauer's work. We shared the subtle feeling of being
the three people in the world that night privileged to be
in the presence. I entertained us all with a recreation of
the scene in the rain with the lovely southern rebel. That

started a sort of anarchic evening of excessive laughter and noisy talk; not the sort of wildness Brandauer was used to.

Before the others arrived, he had carefully measured out his steps around the little folding table, setting down the napkins, measuring the distance between knife and plate, neatly parsing out everything else: the wine in the small, overdecorated hardware-store glasses, the lean anecdotes he told, the chicken casserole he'd cooked, the portion sizes just enough, no more no less.

He was so serious! When he joined in the joke-telling with a story about a Japanese businessman returning home from a trip to an unfaithful wife who had slept with a Jewish man, we laughed and Brandauer laughed. But by departing for a moment from his habitual grave bearing, he gave the joking weight. He was like a Japanese visitor, without the language, trying to join in a lightheartedness he did not quite understand but longed to experience.

During dinner he measured out the food and wine as if we were marooned on a desert island and had to be sure to make the rations last. He'd told me, "I have a bottle," and that's exactly what he had, one bottle of wine for the four of us, not a drop more. You felt he didn't understand why anyone would want more than was enough. And what was enough was clear. His conversation, too, was carefully proportioned—he spoke in short, clear, ironic phrases with not one stammer. And, at one point, when the laughter and noisy commentary got out of hand, loud and boisterous, Brandauer pounded his hand on the table for quiet. A god of large and small universes, he was accustomed to being able to control them; a master of where to place the period, he got his quiet along with a certain astonishment.

About halfway through the interview session before dinner, he suddenly said, "That girl . . . what did you think?"

"I think you're on the spot," I said. "You and Kafka, both. She's one of those tough southern cookies. She expected personal attention and you gave her Kafka."

"I like her intensity," he said. And he quoted Yeats to me—something about lust and rage attending old age.

I said, "How old are you?"

"How much do you weigh?" he said. He'd watched me settle and resettle myself on the couch as I fiddled with the tape recorder. He watched everybody and everything, better at asking than answering questions.

"Too damned much."

And I told him how my second marriage had broken up because in one of my cycles of voracious overeating, I had reached over to my wife's plate, at the Peking Gardens, and started eating from it. Everyone else at the table thought it was mildly amusing, a weird little action. To *her* it meant the marriage was over, it meant I didn't give a damn about anybody or anything except my own hopeless hungers.

"Second wife? You're pretty young."

"I'm on my third."

"Sounds like courses in a meal."

"This is my life we're talking, here," I said. "Don't turn it into another Brandauer metaphor."

"My life," he murmured. "That's what Penelope Anne said. Everybody seems to have this *life* they own." He said it mournfully. I didn't know him well enough to say it wasn't like a car you bought or didn't buy—that he, too, must own a life. But it wasn't that clear.

We finished the interview a few days later and I left Seattle to go back to New York looking for my next job and some fresh ways to patch up the various tears my marriage had developed. I left without finding out what happened to Penelope Anne Golden and her rain-soaked plea for personal literary attention.

I did not see Brandauer again for a year and a half. He was back in his lair, making sentences with which to make stories and making stories in which to nest his sentences. I was busy running around looking for some happiness. I was always able to find *some,* so I could never either renounce the habit or conquer it. I started a magazine designed to appeal to the restless paperback publishing industry, for a time, then did public relations for a ballet company that spun off from the American Ballet Theatre. You get the idea; things that kept me busy but could never be confused with a real career.

Brandauer wrote a letter:

"I read your first novel, *Skydancer.* It is strongly imagined and seriously comic—but is insufficiently crafted so the spirit dies halfway through, leaving the reader with a big chunk of inanimate flesh to deal with. Perhaps you are too scattered to give your craft enough attention. All these different activities." He closed his unexpected letter with a typical Brandauer trick: two quotations without their sources. "Don't forget," he wrote, " 'Life isn't everything.' And in any case 'it's best seen through a single window.' This last—that's what counts."

What the hell did he want? He certainly did not think I could follow him into the compression of despairing images into wildly comic characters which, during these next years, made him as famous as Beckett or Mala-mud—to whom, along with Kafka, he was most often compared. Or into his solitude to become a saint of art. Him and his "that's what counts"—counting up our everlasting pluses and minuses. And what the hell would he do with the sum if he finally arrived at it? In the language of his youth his speed was 78, mine was 33⅓ and often a whirring, laser-spun CD. But I loved his songs. My affection was not unrequited: he invited me to join him at a writers' conference at the University of Arizona in June.

I arrived in Tucson by a series of disastrously late planes. Which is why I missed Brandauer's class and drove up to find him standing surrounded by students in a shimmer of sunshine. I got out of my car and a wall of shaking heat hit my face. Brandauer was the only one who wore a jacket and tie, and he sweated passionately everywhere you could see: his shirt collar wet and limp, his blue tie smeared and wet, his handkerchief mopping eyes and half-bald forehead.

The group thinned out and there was Brandauer with the Angry Young Woman of a year ago: Penelope what-ever-her-name-was. It was the Seattle tableau all over, but instead of rain a monstrous, debilitating fried egg of a sun.

I was so startled to see her that I slowed my approach.

I watched them through a shimmering horizon-haze of crackling, dry heat. It was like a mirage must be, except it didn't look pleasant.

"You're just changing names and places, Penny," I heard Brandauer say. "Sometimes the imagination needs a push."

My God, I thought, a year later and they're still arguing. Though I did note the "Penny." The argument, and who knew what else, had become personal.

"*You* need a push," she said. "Get you out of your damned Kafka-land."

They began to walk. I followed, not wanting to interrupt.

"I'm not telling you how or what to do. But a series of sexual encounters do not make a work of fiction."

"That's because I'm a woman. How about D. H. Lawrence?"

"How about sitting in the shade? I'm fainting from the heat."

"Pricks are okay but cunts are not proper literary material, is that it?"

It was the precise moment to interrupt. Now or never and just in time. Between the two of us we got Brandauer into my air-conditioned Toyota. Tucson in June at 11:30 A.M. Heat stroke was not unthinkable.

We put him to bed in the air-conditioned studio apartment rented for him by the university.

"I should never have come out," he said. "I can't handle you p-p-p-p-people."

I was surprised, again, by the stammer; surprised, too, that he included *me* in his soft, exhausted impeachment.

•

"Okay," Penny said. "He's right." She paused to soak up her second margarita. "My youth is so full of weird sex stuff that I can't make head or tail out of it. But writing stories is the only way I know to get it all straight—if I don't then I'm cooked."

"Right now, *he's* cooked," I said. "And what do you mean, your youth?"

"I'm twenty-four, honey. In Virginia twenty-four is a mature woman." It came out "woeman." And in spite of that lovely lofty white brow and bright red lips, her "honey" was so strongly flavored it shriveled my scrotum.

I took refuge in questions of fact. "How did you get Brandauer to comment on your stories? He was so firm about what he'd do and wouldn't do in the class."

"He insisted I drop out of the class," Penny said. "Disenroll." I swear I had guessed the answer in advance; I was getting to know Brandauer in spite of himself.

"It was the only way to be fair to the others," she said. "I became an auditor and he'd read my stories and go over them with me during lunch."

"Tuna Fish," I said. "Every day."

"How did you know?"

"So you won."

"I lost," she said miserably. "I wanted to exorcise my crazy adolescence by turning it into fiction. He poisoned my hope." Sometimes she just naturally spoke in southern prose, instead of ordinary conversation.

She rummaged in a giant tote bag and out came a notebook. "Here's what he said—it was so awful I had to write it down." She read, like a southern schoolgirl reciting a lesson, *"Art is not ecology. We don't need to conserve the life you've lived and lost—we need a new life from you . . . one you can imagine but probably can't have. We want imagination, not biography. That's what counts."*

She threw the book down and then surprised me by dropping her head on her folded arms. For a full minute she wept. I didn't know what to do, so I reached across the table and touched her cheek. My hand came away wet. It felt too intimate. But it stopped the flood.

She flared up again. "So I said how about Proust? And he said how about you?"

"Why do you care what he thinks so much?" I said hopelessly.

"Because he knows. I didn't mean what I said about pricks and cunts and all that. He's not full of shit. He may be the only one who's not."

Over a Tex-Mex dinner ordered on impulse I tried to distract her. No use.

"How do you make a living in between Brandauer encounters?" I asked.

"Sell books in a little store in downtown Newport News. That's where I first found him."

"Him?"

"His books. When I heard he was going to teach—I grabbed my stories and lit out for the territory. But he wouldn't teach. Just talk about this one crazy story." She poured a ton of ketchup over everything and laughed. "Dug my own grave," she said. "You're a kind man to listen to my troubles." She spoke with that formal prose southerners seem to be born with.

Later we were less formal. I was too close to her, and

she was a mélange of smells; some kind of flowery perfume on her neck, fragrant gin on her breath, and ketchup
on her fingers. Also, the wide blue eyes made things pretty
skittish. Except for Brandauer. We'd made the mistake
of calling to make sure he wasn't dead of heat stroke. He
wasn't, but then he knew Penny and I were together and
it smelled like a betrayal. The night's mission was aborted.

Already I could hear him saying: *"Her eyes—you wanted
to make love to her because of her wide, beautiful eyes—is
that a person, a human being, their eyes, wide or close
together? A human being as parts?"* The Brandauer eye
went right to the heart of things. Butcher of values, he
left no fat on issues—only the hearts of matters were good
enough for him to sell. He respected his customers. Okay,
call them his readers. Call them the audience.

Finally, I understood Brandauer's exasperated stam-
mering wrap-up of Penny and me: "I should never have
left. I can't handle you p-p-p-p-people. . . ." I didn't like
it, but I understood it. Coming out into the world had left
the poor bastard open to everybody from Penny and her
all-important "life" to writing groupies from all over. There
was one young man whose name had been Wilbur Jonas
until he became a convert to Orthodox Judaism. He
changed his name to Chaim and brought his unfinished
novel all the way from the wealth of Shaker Heights
Cleveland, by bus, to Fargo, North Dakota, to hear Brandauer talk about "A Hunger Artist." He had converted
from Jewish Middle-Class Agnosticism to Orthodoxy. His
beard was so long he looked like his own great-grandfa-
ther. Brandauer gave him special attention. He treated
him as if he were some sort of sacred monster.

We were *all* his problems. I who wanted to devour all the life and time there was, and was unable to learn the mysterious Brandauer alchemy of making caterpillars out of butterflies, questions out of answers; Chaim, who wanted to find the Talmudic tradition in new fiction; Penny and the other Pennys who were busy with the sacred matters of personal experience which drew his contempt.

Sometimes I got sick of him.

"What's so special about your buddy the shtetl kid?" I said, irritated. "The Rabbi Nachman of Cleveland. He wouldn't even eat your Tuna Fish, brought his own food? *You* don't believe that stuff," I said. "Why do you give that kid so much leeway?"

"I like Chaim," he said. "I like his choice of names. It affirms Life."

I shrugged. "He wants to bomb Arabs. Some affirmer of life."

"He's fervent," Brandauer said. "That's what counts."

Those years of his coming out were my pendulum years. I swung like a pendulum from Diet Centers to eating binges, from reducing farms to Food City, no doubt making a shambles of my endocrinological system. Jobs were the same. Like Tarzan on his vines I swung my way through the jungle of employment, never staying put very long.

Women, too, were included in this cycle of appetites. At least two of them had wonderfully adhesive skin—that is, they stuck to my life. Others had skin as smooth as a mind without memory and soon became part of the past. One of them, Sybil, became my third wife. I wanted

Brandauer to be the best man but I was afraid he already was, and skipped the invitation.

One November, at a conference in Fargo, North Dakota, Brandauer told me, "You're a feverish man. A cooler temperature would be more productive." I allowed myself an intimate moment with the Master.

"The fever is not the problem," I said. And I tried to make him understand how it was always the matter at hand, whatever it is, which heated me up—a lovely woman who promised understanding and pleasure, not necessarily in that order; a *poulet à l'estragon avec moutarde et endives;* and that fine literary moment when the word "and" joins the actions of two characters perfectly. All were equal in me.

Brandauer gazed at me in spectacled despair. His silhouette seemed more fragile than ever; his cheeks were sinking inwards, signs of age or loss of weight, I couldn't tell.

"That's only good for somebody who's going to live forever," he said. "I haven't met one yet. The rest of us have to choose."

"How about a walk?" I said, desperately.

"This is North Dakota. It's five degrees outside."

"Ah," I said. "Yes. As usual I forgot."

The following summer we met at the Bennington conference. I was in my brief phase of smoking good cigars— delicious, slow-smoking, fragrant panatelas made by

Upmann in Havana, shipped, legally, to Switzerland to a man named Gross, who then shipped them to me, illegally, in a box marked *Swiss Cigars: Gift Under Twenty-five Dollars.*

"Is it worth all that trouble," Brandauer asked.

"Absolutely."

"I think maybe the trouble is part of the pleasure. It makes a big deal out of a small joy."

To throw him off the scent I told him about Hemingway's comment that you had to plan your pleasures, work at them—otherwise they wouldn't happen. Everything else will happen anyway, work, obligations, but not pleasures, unless you planned for them.

I leaned back satisfied with having scored. Brandauer stood up, said, "It goes vice versa, too," and went home to his desk. As if to prove him right, I wasted that entire day in pointless phone calls, switching vacation plans, while he wrote a page and a half.

A couple of years later I was asked to fill in at the last minute, at a winter conference in Boulder, Colorado. I was working at a new job: writer/producer of trailers for monster movies. You know, bite-sized smorgasbords designed to make children and certain minority groups—the primary monster-lovers—hungry for the movie itself. I needed the money to pay for alimony. The divorce from Sybil had turned into the usual horror movie and I'd put on thirty pounds out of misery.

But Brandauer was going to be in Boulder, so I cleared

my schedule. When I arrived, there he was, small green-
covered Modern Library edition of the selected Kafka
stories in hand.

In the interim he had won the Pulitzer Prize for his
collected stories and a National Book Award for a new
novel. The novels were getting shorter and shorter. You
could hardly tell them from the stories, which were
also getting smaller. I was eager to see him. But more
eager to have *him* see *me*. I'd just dropped forty-seven
pounds at the Pritikin Center in Florida. It had cost
all my extra cash—but I was proud of the exhibition of
will.

There was a foot of snow everywhere. We met for lunch
in some western inn-type place with a fireplace, and a
moosehead on the wall. They featured steaks and veni-
son, but I knew what Brandauer was up for. I took perverse pleasure in ordering even less. What's less than Tuna
Fish on white toast and a cup of black coffee? It wasn't
easy, but I scrounged up an assorted vegetable plate. That
got his attention. But he made no comment.

"I brought you a present," I told him. "It's a poem. I
wrote it on eight hundred calories a day at Pritikin. It's
called 'The Hunger Artist.' "

It was a long son of a bitch but he seemed to pay special attention to the last two stanzas.

> Out of the fleshly fabrication
> Appears an honesty of skin.
> In the hungry, human situation
> The gotten grace is always thin.

The body less than fills the eye,
The flesh, a tissue shield.
Bare bones beneath a cannibal sky:
Shape is fate revealed.

"It's not 'The Hunger Artist,' it's 'A Hunger Artist.' "
He folded the gift-poem carefully in four parts and put it
in his wallet. "The article is crucial. He's a special case."

Not a word about my poem, a poem as personal to me
as my gut.

We stormed the snow a blast of white wind in our
faces and walked to the parking lot. I had to shout to be
heard.

"Okay," I said, off balance as only he could throw me
off, "The—A—My God . . . I've heard you read that story
in eight cities to students dying to learn how to write their
own stories . . ."

"Are you finished with your new book?"

"No—I've been gearing up for this new job. And the
divorce took it out of me."

"Ah," he said. There was nothing more devastating
than a Brandauer "Ah."

"Do you like making these commercials you work at?"

As if confessing something shameful I said: "I do, yes.
It's fun, it's easy, and it's good money."

He fiddled with the lock to his car.

"It may be frozen," I said. "Let me try."

He paused a long time and said, "I could never handle
the world the way you do." This did not sound as if he
admired me for it, believe me.

Irritably, I said, "I think *you* do it much better. The

world handles me, not vice versa. I'm always playing catch-up with money and women."

"Thanks for the poem," he said.

Before I could reply with something properly bitter, the snowy shape of Penelope Anne Golden made its way through a blast of white wet. She wore a hooded parka; the hood made her look like one of those figures in a medieval print; all she needed was a scythe.

I figured we were finished, so I backed away as she approached. I watched them from the safety of my warming car. She was gesticulating wildly, Brandauer stood there like a prisoner being accused of various crimes. Every few moments he shrugged. I don't think he said anything. Clearly, he still had not treated her "life" the way she wished.

I started the car and Penelope was standing outside knocking on the window. She spat a mouthful of snow at me. When I rolled the window down she stuck her sweet snowy face in and kissed me. It was an angry kiss, more like a bite.

"Do y'all want to make love to me?" she asked.

It was such a crazed moment that I thought the "y'all" meant both of us—me and poor soaked Brandauer hunching himself into his Volkswagen. But it was nothing so fancy. He must have said something about her stories that got her southern rage going and I was handy. Her mouth had a soft wet give that was tempting. But over her shoulder I saw Brandauer struggling to start his frozen car and all I could do was shake my head from side to side.

"Fuck you," she said and stumbled away in the snow.

•

The next day, in class, Brandauer read the last line of my poem: "Shape is fate revealed."

"What the hell was that?" I said, afterwards.

"It seemed appropriate."

"You're too damned appropriate, Brandauer," I said. "That line makes no sense without the rest of the poem."

"Too bad," he said. "You gave it to me. It's mine now. And I gave it to the class. Remember it's *A* not *The*. By the way, you look terrific with your new shape. Maybe now you can make do with less all around."

I said nothing about yesterday's craziness in the snow with Penelope. He said even less.

A few months later *Time* magazine got wind of Brandauer's cross-country number. It was oddball enough to get their attention. This shy master suddenly zipping around the country teaching writing students using only a fourteen-page story about a strange custom of fasting as an art form. And, of course, Kafka was the perfect writer to refer to without having to read him. Everybody knows what you mean when you talk about Kafka, don't they?

When they called me the researcher said they'd gotten my name from a Ms. Penelope Anne Golden. I thought, she doesn't know the rules of the game, and eased them off the phone. Naturally they confused Brandauer with the Hunger Artist in the story. And naturally they called it *"The* Hunger Artist," losing Brandauer's precious *A.*

Reading the piece made me think about our singular friendship. What a match! Brandauer owned a natural dignity and carried himself with such care that it bordered on the mysterious. He had the patience of someone enrolled in a religious order for life whose faith had never been shaken. Myself, I had a gift for clowning and an attention span of about a minute and a half. He was at home with order, I was companion to confusion. His arena of pleasures was narrow, carefully attended to. Mine was indiscriminate loose (with significant exceptions such as ignoring Penelope Anne's sexual invitation). And, strangest of all, he insisted on taking me seriously; something I could never quite manage. We were a comic pairing, a Mutt and Jeff of the writing life.

The comedy ended abruptly in Miami. There was a woman at his bedside, tall, European-looking, her dress a little too long, all in gray. She fluttered off the instant I arrived.

". . . who told you . . . ?"

"Don't talk."

"Isn't it crazy dying *here?* Did you see those foolish-looking palm trees on the way from the airport? This is not a serious place."

He was bringing his own seriousness with him, hooked up to all the usual hi-tech medical paraphernalia, a Frankenstein monster of unexpected disaster.

"The food is terrible here."

"Hospitals," I said stupidly.

"It's Tuna Fish every day for lunch. Awful."

He didn't seem to know he was making his own deathbed comedy. Maybe they gave him Tuna Fish because someone told them it was his lifelong lunch.

Brandauer gestured for me to bend closer. His chest-wind was not blowing with its usual strength.

"Chaim . . ."

"No, I'm . . ."

"I know, I know." He was irritated at his lapse—confusing me with his Orthodox Jewish disciple. He wanted order, as usual, not confusion.

"I envy the p-p-p-p-p-" It was the longest, most painful stammer I'd ever heard from him. I waited while he struggled. Finally the word arrived. ". . . panther!" We were back to topic A. Or topic K. Relieved and exhausted by the effort he added, "I envy him—just a little," and sneaked in a quick little smile. "That girl, Penelope . . . you slept with her?"

"No," I said too quickly.

"Ah," he said. "Too bad."

I was starved. In the gray hospital cafeteria I drank some chemical coffee and ate a cardboard croissant. The pale bird of a woman who had been at Brandauer's bedside sat down next to me.

"No intrusion meant," she said. "But you're a friend of my husband's, are you not?"

She spoke with a foreign accent and sounded like a

translation, and that was how I learned the whole secret subtext of Brandauer's story, a wife and a son kept hidden in Italy all those years. Her name was Francesca and her son was Mauro. She was content, she quickly made it clear, to be Brandauer's background story. Her son had been left with friends in Genoa. But she'd sought me out because she wanted the world to know that her husband was honest and responsible and had always taken care of them even during his long absences.

"What can I do?" I asked.

What came through at last was that, to her, I was Brandauer's friend the journalist. He must have shown her the interview in the *Paris Review*, so many years ago.

"Tell me," I said, "has he had this heart problem for a long time?"

"He found out about twelve years ago," she said. "His whole family had the heart—but his started then."

"I see." I don't know what I saw, but twelve years ago was when he'd left his little room to start teaching.

"And you will tell how he was good and a good father, too. Not just a writer. You will write about this for the world."

I was too exhausted to set her straight, too miserable at how awfully ill, white of face, and starved Brandauer looked. Yes, I would tell the whole world, I said, I would tell how fine and honest he was. What the hell! The comedy of misunderstanding had begun with a generation of students excitedly greeting Brandauer and, instead, getting Kafka. Let it end—if it was ending—with a redundant, foolish promise. I had no means of addressing any large public to tell them about this man who was, indeed, so fine and honest that he sometimes seemed a visitor from a different place. She kissed me on the cheek and left an odor of dried flowers, vaguely foreign.

"What I couldn't tell Penny was . . ." He started on this as soon as I was at his bedside again, as if we'd been talking all along. ". . . she couldn't see it . . . that putting it together was the main thing . . . all the big chunks of life she had . . . all the struggles, the pleasures . . . you need a line, I told her . . . a line of words . . . just like a poet you need a line . . . then the people and the lives and what they do to each other . . . then they can go into the line and find their beat . . . But . . ."

"Listen," I said. "How do you feel? Do you want the nurse?"

I waited. He seemed to have forgotten I was there. Then, very softly:

"Enough . . . and not one bit more. That's what counts." He laughed. It was like a cough with an edge of amusement.

"Isn't that what you've been telling *me* all this time?" I felt like an idiot dealing myself in. It seemed to me that he nodded.

"But don't forget," I said. "For the panther enough is a whole lot of bloody meat."

Brandauer smiled. "Did I tell you how I envied the p-p-p-p-"

This time I interrupted and supplied the word. "Yes, the panther," I said. It sounded impatient and mean-spirited. I felt badly that I had not let him finish his own stammer and I began a burst of words. "I've always loved the double ending: when the Hunger Artist dies after whispering that the public should not admire him. . . . *I have to fast, I can't help it . . . I couldn't find the food I liked. If I had found it, believe me, I should have made no fuss and stuffed myself like you or anyone else. . . .*" I was weirdly proud at being able to quote so much from memory. Foolishly, as if that meant I understood it, understood Brandauer, our confused friendship, my eternally unfinished life.

"Then they clear out the cage," I went on, "and put in the young panther. *The food he liked was brought him without hesitation by the attendants . . . his noble body, furnished almost to the bursting point with all that it needed, seemed to carry freedom around with it too. . . .*" I was quoting more and more, in desperation, watching Brandauer fade away from me on the rumpled pillow. After all the years of his classes it was a final examination I'd suddenly set for myself.

"*. . . somewhere in his jaws it seemed to lurk; and the joy of life streamed with such ardent passion from his throat that for the onlookers it was not easy to stand the shock of it. But they braced themselves, crowded round the cage, and did not want ever to move away.*"

"Bravo, my friend," Brandauer said, although I'd done nothing more than quote the published ending. Perhaps I'd passed the examination.

"I wonder," he said, "if panthers have heart attacks . . . all that red meat . . ." At the corner of my eye I saw his wife start to move towards us.

"Listen," he said, already fainter.

"Yes . . ."

"That thing you wrote—the gift—a poem about dieting . . ."

"Yes."

"Well." Brandauer paused and a shadow of an old smile showed up on his lips.

"It doesn't matter so much what you eat," he said. *What matters is what eats you. That's what . . ."* Apparently he could not manage the last "counts"; the last summation left hanging in the strange hospital air. He grew silent and the silence became sleep and the sleep became death but not until the next morning while I was turning my rented Ford onto its side at the entrance to the freeway.

"What did he mean, that stuff about the Panther?" Penny asked.

"Who, Kafka?" I was in a teasing mood. My ribs had stopped aching, though they were still strapped. The cuts on my forehead had healed. I'd survived.

"Brandauer, I mean," she said. "You know damned well."

"I think the talk about the Panther was for himself," I told her. "There was something else for you and a few things for me."

She laughed. Not an angry note in her scale these days. "He's preaching at me from beyond the you-know-what."

"Talking, maybe—preaching, no!"

I was determined to be serious for as long as possible, determined to hold out for as long as possible against the white dress, the white skin, the shining pearls sliding across the summer suntan, the sweet citrus scent of perfume. I told her what Brandauer had said about the trick of just enough and no more—about the line of words, though I couldn't get it exactly as he'd said it.

We were in Middletown, Connecticut, in July, a hot and sticky time in the Connecticut River Valley. The Wesleyan Writers' Conference, like so many, was scheduled for a hellish time of the year. I'd called her to deliver Brandauer's message and to ask her if she was still coming to the conference even though our original reason for enrolling was now cremated, the ashes buried in a cemetery in Italy.

And here we were, wearing our name tags but skipping the standard get-acquainted cocktail party in favor of our own dinner. We sat at the bar waiting for a table and I told her about the accident, about the turbaned Dr. Singh at the emergency room, about how he had ignored my Brandauer-grief and blamed the crash on vertigo and weakness due to my crazy up-and-down dieting.

Tonight, I said, was definitely to be up. The place I'd picked was famous for its lamb, its fresh vegetables, and its strawberry soufflé dessert, which had to be ordered hours before dinner. I'd done that and with it a rich '79 Château LaLagune.

Penny said, "Do you think he knew you'd hunt me up and deliver his last words?"

"I don't know. He didn't have too much breath left and he knew it. He was just getting all sorts of stuff out. Last Chance Saloon stuff."

"I kept thinking he'd drop that damned story. Pay

attention to something else. It doesn't matter anymore."
She laughed. "God, we fought it out in rain and heat and
snow."

"What *were* you two fighting about?"

"I thought I knew—I wanted him to pay attention to
me and my life—my love affairs in purple prose . . . yes,
I know that's what they were, now . . . I wanted him to
love my stories as if they were parts of my body, of my
self. Then, when that didn't happen and he stuck to his
guns about making me imagine everything as if it was
new, then I wanted him to love me and my body as if we
were my writing. But he wouldn't do that, either. All he
would do was tell me to cool out my prose, cool out my
life . . . cool . . . God!"

"Was that about when you asked me if I wanted to
make love to you in a blizzard in North Dakota or somewhere? I figured that for a ricochet."

"Did I do that?" It was the first time I'd ever seen the
southern steamroller embarrassed. I did not remind her
about the "Fuck you" that had followed. "I was so pissed
off I told *Time* magazine all sorts of bullshit about him."

"I noticed."

"There's too much air conditioning in here," she said.
But the maître d' quickly rescued her from embarrassment and chill.

Dinner was phenomenal—the lamb pink and juicy and
the soufflé hot and runny. Her big theory came out over
the coffee.

"If you hadn't called me I would have dug *you* up."

"Oh?"

"I had to tell you what I'd figured out about Brandauer. When I found out about the heart attack it threw me. After I stopped crying I read the full obit and a light bulb went off." She leaned over the debris of dinner, intent in the old way, almost angry again. *"He knew he was going to die,"* she said. "The paper said he'd had a history of heart trouble for more than a decade. It explains everything."

She was in no mood for my interruption or disclaimer. "His picking that particular story and living the way he did, the way he gave only the minimum necessary to life and *everything* to writing."

"Because he knew his clock was ticking so fast, you mean?"

"Don't forget," she said solemnly, "the only piece that you could call furniture in the Hunger Artist's cage was a clock."

"My God," I said. "You're picking up where he left off."

"That's why Brandauer kept teaching that story. It was his anthem." She wiped some pink from her lips, soufflé or lipstick I couldn't tell.

"That's not all," she said.

"Hold it," I said. "He could just as easily have gone the other way. You know—live all you can—that Henry James stuff . . . seize the carpe . . . carpe the diem . . ."

"Ha, ha," she said. "Listen—I've got something I want to read to you." I'd never read or heard anything she'd written. She pulled out some crumpled papers and over the coffee cups and breadcrumbs she read this:

KRAKAUER: *a story*

Word was out that Krakauer was leaving his cage. After fourteen years of writing private astonishments, he was going into the public world to teach. This was an event worthy of comment in media as disparate as the *New York Times Magazine* (with its oddly inappropriate ads of young women in their sensual underwear) and *Critical Inquiry*, with its puritanically ordered columns of dense text.

Would he teach hermeneutics and literature—the Real Stuff—or just creative writing, the Fake Stuff? Would he be skinny, emaciated from years of isolation in Genoa, making and remaking sentences? the *New York Times* wondered. Would he be distracted from the larger concerns of the Academy by the sophomoric demands of students? *Critical Inquiry* speculated.

On a spring day in Seattle, the mystery was dispelled. That first morning Krakauer met with a crowded class of students still wet behind the ears with Seattle rain.

"I will not read any students' stories," he announced, this wraith from the lost land of language. "Instead, I will read 'A Hunger Artist' by Franz Kafka."

Muted exclamations of pain and thwarted personal ambition. One pale young woman felt her chance at a new life slipping away.

Krakauer was firm. He began to read. . . .

It was too damned good; the sentences supple and simple. Better than what I've written here. Tougher, more condensed, cooler; less tangled with the ego of a narrative voice.

"Hey," I said. "I haven't read your other stuff. But you seem to have cooled out. It's very strong, so far."

"I know," she said folding the papers back into her bag. "It's just the beginning."

I decided that such an expansive dinner deserved a cigar and we moved to the terrace.

"Do you mind if I smoke this?"

"Go on. My daddy smoked cigars."

I touched Penny's cheek and rubbed my hand gently downwards, to see if anything had changed between us. She closed those enormous eyes for a flick of the lids. Her tongue licked a raspberry seed from her upper lip. A tick of time but it told me enough.

"Well," I said. "I guess it's just us, now."

A long sigh, then a grin. "I miss him," she said. "Even more than when he was here."

Melancholy laughter from both of us.

I put my arm around her shoulder and she collapsed against me. I had a story to finish on my desk, that night. It could wait.

In the morning I woke with my head on Penny's gently moving stomach. I felt satisfied and hungry and strange. The night before we'd been a kind of solution for each other. Now it was morning and we could start the natural process of becoming problems for each other. What would we do now with our bodies, our minds, our stories? How would we deal with each other—our anxieties, our appetites? *It doesn't matter what you eat. It matters what eats you. That's what . . .*

Penny stirred. She got up and went to the bathroom. When she came out I watched her while she performed a morning stretch, warm and lean. Conventional southern young woman that she was, she'd worn a white nightgown to bed, like a bride. The sun shone behind her through the bathroom window and I saw her shape revealed through the fabric of her nightgown, her parted legs an elegant V with curly pubic hair, perfectly clear, infinitely mysterious. My desire for her was urgent and stupid, without thought. I had no wish to read her stories, to encounter previous lovers. I wanted to be Opus One. I made love to her as if I wanted to get her inside myself, not the other way around. The exertion stung my strapped ribs and reminded me of my brush with highway death following my final brush with Brandauer. But holding Penny afterwards made me feel safe for the moment. I noticed, for the first time, that her right eye sort of wandered. Fresh details; she would be my newest unfinished story.

Immediately after, she was back at her *idée fixe*. She sat up straight. "Now, in the morning light," she said, "do you see how it explains everything. He *knew* he was going to die."

I kissed her lips; a faint flavor of raspberry from the night before. "You mean unlike the rest of us."

"Come on. You know what I mean."

"No," I said, implacable, remembering the jaws of the panther.

Sunday Morning
by Wallace Stevens

(a Story by Daniel Stern)

WHEN Osterweil finished teaching the Stevens class he knew with an absolute certainty that he was going to die and he set out to find the piece of music that he wanted played at his funeral. Not just the particular piece, but the one recorded performance that would suffice, and no other.

This confirmation of his death did not refer to that precise moment, just some day; not the present, the future, even perhaps the distant future. Nor was it the general knowledge which everyone shares and dips into now and then—the kind of mortality-nudge which only makes present life more delicious. This was more like some weird gnostic gift of the coming event; closer to an experienced conviction than abstract information, and it surprised the hell out of him. He just saw himself dead and that was that!

In the morning Osterweil had woken up anxious about his afternoon class—in particular his upcoming usual skirmish with Rowena Ralph. He was also anxious about the annual picnic of his narrow, intense group of friends, scheduled that evening, for the Santa Monica Park. Lorelei, Kessler, Stepner, and French—a mixture of business people, professionals, and one doctor, Stepner—they cherished their circle of friendship as a precious geometric invention, and the annual picnic was a central ritual, never to be missed. The night before, the weather report had predicted wild, lashing rains and unpredictable thunder and lightning. He felt awful about the picnic turning into such an experience—and worse about the possible cancellation of the event. Since his divorce he'd cherished an almost mystical concern over his connections with friends. As if *they* were now his aborted marriage and his delayed and then unarrived children.

All this was actually an improvement over recent awakenings. He had been having early-morning incidents of what he called his "Thanatosis."

"What's that?" Nina had asked. "Sounds like the title of an old poem."

"I guess it's sadness masquerading under a sense of being mortal."

Osterweil gave her the lightweight treatment. Confessing to excessive brooding about death was like admitting a drinking problem, or drugs—a weakness you couldn't control. He'd found it easier to simply tell his recent ex that he was feeling a little down. He certainly didn't want to let her into the extended fantasy life he called his Thanatosis.

"For God's sake, you're a DJM," Nina had said, impatient with her past, that is, with Osterweil. "That's the acronym in the personals in the *New York Review of Books*. It's not such a bad thing to be, living in Los Angeles. A Divorced Jewish Male. I suppose that's not really an acronym because it's unpronounceable. Maybe you're just still down about *us.*"

"It's not unpronounceable. It's unspeakable," Osterweil said. "And I'm *not* still down about you."

"I said 'us.' "

"Same thing. It's just life and time," he'd said and left it at that. Nina was a tax lawyer; rationality was her religion. She believed in psychoanalysis but not in the unconscious. He could never figure her out. It wouldn't have helped to tell her that he'd gone from giving a eulogy for a friend killed in a freak car crash on the San Diego Freeway to being asked to make the arrangements for the funerals of two colleagues, one very old, one quite young, and from there to a snowballing sequence of death-related imaginations. He had begun to improvise eulogies, to choose appropriate musical selections and quotations for friends, often while shaving—the problem being that some of these friends were still alive. He tried to keep some control by making sure that they were either old or sick; but he ran out of those pretty quickly and had to resort to the merely middle-aged. And in the latest escalation he had been imagining his *own* last rites.

The latest nuance was his browsing among the great works of music for exactly the right selection to be played when he could no longer hear it. It was a strange training for the ear—to hear the ineffable, or to hear through the ears of others, his mourning family and friends. Which ears: Lorelei, with her austere love for German art songs, or Stepner, who, frankly, preferred pop classics? It must be what composers have to do, he thought. Listen through the imaginary ears of others. Poets, too. He would find a way to use all this in one of his classes. That would take some of the pain out.

Osterweil was a former poet. Not a failed poet or a poet manqué; former. To be a failed poet you had to keep making poems, and he had not. To be a would-be poet you had to yearn but never perform. He had performed, had judged himself not first-rate, and had stopped.

Instead, he taught poets who *were* first-rate. He had also turned to athletics: running and working out. Giving up the possibility of making poetry and making more of his body were somehow connected. And both, weirdly, connected to his divorce from Nina. "Weirdly" is the word, because he felt, yet could not map out, these connections. What the hell, he thought, I'm a teacher, not an electrician.

"You're the doctor," he said in one of his odd, imaginary, bathroom-mirror conversations. This one was in the office of Dr. Owens, his internist.

"Ah, yes," Owens said, pen in hand, poised over Osterweil's open chart, "Thanatosis. Inflammation of the death instinct, the way cirrhosis is an inflammation of the liver?" He looked up at the imaginary Osterweil. "There's a lot of that going around."

"Aha?"

"Especially in your demographic group?"

"What's that?"

"DJM. How old are you?"

"Thirty-eight."

"Perfect."

"What do you mean?"

Silence.

The imaginary conversation was mildly comforting. Osterweil had the sense that what he was experiencing was somehow "unmanly." It was better to think of it in medical terms, though that was also slightly comical.

And that was as far as he'd gotten. What had come next was Rowena Ralph, his tormentor in Modernism in Poetry: 108. Here, of course, his fantasies had all kinds of models to work from. In every class Rowena Ralph, who had blond braids, like her namesake in Ivanhoe, was determined to find the transcendental. This was okay in Whitman; it was all right, now and then, in Robert Frost. But they were doing Wallace Stevens and she had locked horns in a death struggle with Osterweil over his interpretations of Stevens as a poet of the earth, of the here and now, of weather and the sun. She wanted Heavens and Gods complete with capitalized G's. And when Stevens spoke of "an evening without angels" she demanded an ironic subtext in which he really meant *with* angels. She was driving him over the edge on which he was already poised.

He'd even begun to notice the insulting, sensual way her skirts folded between her long legs, clinging to one or the other of her thighs. Now Osterweil was no ancient German professor out of an old movie, *The Blue Angel*, ready to be senselessly tormented by the frustration of his senses. Before marrying Nina, he'd had a few affairs with ex-students; and had once actually been brought up on charges of sexual harassment—though unjustly—by a strange southern sophomore. He was quickly cleared. "One of us is crazy," he'd told Nina. "And it's not me."

Still, the last time, after tangling with Rowena's snotty theological questions to the amusement of the other students, he'd found himself watching to see which way the skirt would fall; which thigh would win the toss. And in confusion had ended the class ten minutes early, announcing:

"Please read 'Sunday Morning' before the next clash."

Rolling waves of laughter followed by Osterweil's flight.

Thus, the background of Osterweil's significant day. Awakening to anxieties about picnics, thighs, thunderstorms, and poems he tried to calm himself the only way he knew, by reading. Sweetened coffee rolling in his mouth, he opened a book at random, *The Journals of Emerson.* His mood was so low that even as he did this he thought how damned bookish he was. A drowning man gazing with contempt at his own life-jacket. Nevertheless, he read Emerson's entry:

Crossing a bare common, in snow puddles, at twilight, under a clouded sky, without having in my thoughts any occurrence of special good fortune, I have enjoyed a perfect exhilaration. I am glad to the brink of fear.

And stopped, stunned.

Glad to the brink of fear. The image was astonishing, instantly convincing. This was the other side of his bookishness—the always present possibility of coming on a book, a chapter, a miraculous sentence, a phrase—like "glad to the brink of fear." He had lived that phrase in his gut a time or two. The tenth day of a ten-day holiday in Venice during which each day was flooded with a beneficence of sunshine and he or Nina would flip the shutters of their little room in the Hotel Londra which gave out onto the quai, in the morning to open the floodgates to bright yellow and rose colors and the sounds of a thousand nuns and Japanese tourists pouring onto the Piazetta, cameras ready to record the perfection of weather, of paintings, of brilliant light on water and later of shadowed, latticed late-afternoon light on the same canal. Each day was a gift of the sun made to the supple water which the two of them, after ten days, took for granted as their own.

By the third day he had cautiously allowed himself to feel the gladness, no other word would do. It wasn't happiness because that implied continuation, and it wasn't ecstasy because that implied brevity. No, it was entirely a being glad, and by the time they'd gotten to the last day, Osterweil *was* glad to the brink of fear. Not then, he hadn't known that, but now, now reading Emerson's words about twilight and snow puddles in Boston, he knew he had been so glad that it terrified him for his life. The gladness was so intense that it made him feel in his bones, in his stomach, the seat of panic, that such gladness must end, might even be forgotten, and then perhaps everything might end and could be forgotten—and facing the job of defining that "everything," Osterweil had given up.

So much for honeymoons and gladness.

There were other occasions, too, which echoed to Emerson's words, but Osterweil had no need to rehearse them. The thrill of the phrase, of the whole journal entry, was enough to send him off to his Modernism in Poetry 108 with anxiety calmed, for the moment, hope rising in the east, heavy with memories of the Venetian Empire. Rowena Ralph, watch out!

Outside, the air was a warm soup, the kind of atmosphere inviting to enormous flashes of sudden lightning. The kind which could—he thought in his present agitated mood—instantly fry friends celebrating an annual rite of companionship in open air. He'd often complained to Nina that she'd brought them west to a place with a strange, sometimes pleasant flow of air but with absolutely no weather. It felt like a strange destiny for Osterweil, devotee of Wallace Stevens, poet of the sun, moon, ocean, mortality, but above all, of weather.

Rowena's skirts were back in slippery action along with her insistent challenges from the heavens. The class settled back, detached but alert, like seconds in a duel. Osterweil had just finished an impassioned statement about the woman in "Sunday Morning," idly daydreaming amid her oranges, near her green cockatoo, about eternity and/or Christianity, when Rowena stood up— stood up on long, rustle-skirted legs—and quoted:

> *"She says, 'But in contentment I still feel*
> *The need of some imperishable bliss.' "*

Long pause. Osterweil: "Yes, Miss Ralph?"

"Don't you see?"

"Not yet!"

"Well, it's like Ralph Waldo Emerson . . ."

Osterweil held his breath. He was normally a perfectly good breather, but for an instant *not* breathing was the only natural response. She was reading his mind the way, that morning, he had read Emerson's. He shut up.

She went on. "Everyone thinks Emerson is this terrific humanist, a Unitarian minister and all, when all the time he's really longing for a happiness that's"—she blew the word at Osterweil like a sibilant bubble—*"Transcendent."*

Later he would convince himself that it was coincidence. Though the argument from Emerson was flawed, it wasn't from Mars! Just, a weak comparison. He did a verbal dance through the rest of the class and, somehow, at the end, Rowena Ralph was silenced. Later he would remember the duologue as kind of simplistic duel, reduced to two statements: Rowena was trying to tell him he would not actually die and he firmly maintained that he would. This was never said. But Osterweil took everything personally, the most abstract philosophical and theological questions, or which movie to see on a particular evening out. It used to drive Nina crazy. Now it was doing the same to him.

After Osterweil's last statement, Rowena closed up shop and no longer gave Osterweil parry for thrust. The duel was over and the class burst into applause. That was when the certainty of his own death crawled into his soul and made a nest for itself, comfortable, as if it would never leave. By being right, by being true to his own convictions, by refusing Rowena's heaven on behalf of Wallace Stevens, he'd condemned himself. All that was left for him was to go and search out the perfect piece of music to be played at the final ceremony.

Rowena Ralph crossed her legs with a silken slither.

He was quite sure it had to be Gilels playing the Beethoven Opus 111 piano sonata—the C minor; the second movement, the theme and variations. If any one piece of music could give the end of a life the strength of a spiritual adventure then *this* piece could; these adventures of that simplest of three note themes elaborated into a passionate series of transformations were what he had to have on that final occasion of his presence, or first occasion of his absence. Whichever.

It seemed imperative to get the recording at once. Of course it was an old recording, but they were always reissuing the Golden Oldies. Into his car and off down Sunset Boulevard towards—towards where? He'd not bought a single record in the eighteen months since Nina had gotten her big chance and come to the Los Angeles firm—Gardner and Lily—trailing Osterweil behind her. His only defense, as usual, had been a joke: "Why go? You'll never make partner. Clearly they're going to pick someone named Flowers. *Gardner, Lily and Flowers, good morning.*" But they'd gone, jokes and all, newly married, newly transplanted, and now newly divorced. Very Los Angeles, all this "new" stuff.

In New York he would have known where to go. Old records were to be found at Record Hunter and there were all the little dusty shops in the Village with 78s and recordings of Bartók playing Debussy, that kind of thing. Even Sam Goody's might have done the trick. There was undoubtedly a Sam Goody's in L.A. and any rational person would have simply checked the Yellow Pages before dashing into the car and onto Sunset Boulevard. But this was not a rational moment, this was the first day of the rest of his death.

Osterweil turned on the radio with an automatic hand.

KFAC—the L.A. version of WNYC. And in a few moments heard, as from a voice in the heavens—after all where *was* radio if not in the heavens?—"Call the CD Hotline with any questions about compact discs." *Was* it on a compact disc? Osterweil's rough time sense told him that Gilels was sixties and seventies and compact discs were eighties and nineties. But he'd often heard the phrase "digitally remastered" without the slightest idea of what it might mean. Who knew what happy surprises technology held for him on this awful day?

He pulled over at a street-corner phone on Santa Monica Boulevard. The relentlessly courteous voice on the phone told him that the recording he wanted was Deutsche Grammophon #2GH419174.

"No," the salesman said. He was a young man with the music student look you want in these situations. "That number would be Opus 110. A-flat major. Not C minor."

"That's not the one I want."

"Well, there are other performances of the one-eleven. How about Horowitz."

"It has to be Gilels."

The young man nodded seriously, willing to go along with Osterweil for a moment. "That's a pretty rare recording, you know. Gilels recorded very little Beethoven—he did Scriabin, Liadow, Tchaikovsky. You know where they might have a copy—the Musical Gryphon over on Sepulveda. Let me give 'em a call."

Osterweil breathed better. The famous much-joked-about Los Angeles courtesy was about to pay off. And the voice from the Musical Gryphon assured the young man that they did indeed have a copy and would hold it in the name of Osterweil. Even the wet, subtropical air which flowed around Osterweil as he got into his car could not dampen his excitement.

But the man behind the counter at the second store was not young, did not seem like a music student. He was more like a man who'd spent his youth and all his hopes playing unaccompanied Bach on the cello and now, middle-aged, in disappointment and irony, sold records.

"We don't have it," he said, a flat midwestern negative.

Osterweil felt himself sweating. He had a swift sense that this was getting out of hand, and yet he could not stop himself.

"But the guy called from Goody's. His name was Al—Al Rose."

"Not me he didn't."

"Well, who was on duty before you?"

"This is a small store, mister. The manager covered for me on my lunch break."

"Aha!"

"What are you, a cop?"

"Is the manager here?"

"MR. LEVINE!"

Mr. Levine was managerial, that is, he wanted to make everyone happy. But he had, it seemed, just sold that very recording to someone else.

"But you told the man at Goody's you'd hold it in my name—Osterweil. That's a pretty weird coincidence," Osterweil said. He felt the close encroachments of paranoia.

"Well," Mr. Levine said, and leaned on the counter in

frankness, "the fact is, this person didn't ask for that particular record. I forgot about the name and I just assumed, you know, because of getting that call from Al Rose at Goody's that the next customer who talked about Beethoven was you. So I let loose with a lot of my enthusiasm for late Beethoven—and this customer, who actually shops here a lot, got kind of excited about the idea of Gilels and that spectacular second movement—the theme and variations. Sorry."

My God, Osterweil thought, could everybody read his mind today? Rowena Ralph with her Emerson, Mr. Levine with his theme and variations. What was going on? To stall, he took a swerve. "One-eleven is not really late," Osterweil declaimed. "Late starts with Opus 127, the earliest."

He knew he was simply being irritable and contentious. Who the hell knew exactly where late anything began or ended. Well, no, ended you could obviously tell, but beginnings were not so simple. He was just angry at getting this close to the prize, even though there was no real reason he had to have this particular recording today.

"Listen," Osterweil said, joining Levine's arms on the counter. *"I have to have this particular recording, today!"*

The manager rummaged, randomly, among catalogues and sales slips. It was the kind of rummaging people do before making that sudden phone call to the police.

"Look," Osterweil said, "I know it sounds crazy, but music is a deeply personal thing. You understand that."

Levine nodded solemnly. His jury was clearly still out regarding who was being deeply personal or just crazy.

"If you could tell me the name of the person you sold it to . . ."

Levine's head swung, like a tolling bell, from left to right. Silence.

"I'll double what they paid." Osterweil took the next step into hysteria. Nina had always accused him of spraying any little extra money every which way. "This is crazy," he heard Nina's cool, sensible voice say. "There must be . . ."

"There must be some other recording that will do." Levine was softening. It was an unsatisfactory suggestion but it was better than the police.

"Here's Gina Bachauer. Also a digital remastering of a great old performance."

Osterweil's silence made it clear that they were coming to the end of a road. But Levine started his rummaging number again and Osterweil panicked and recovered enough to begin to weave a romantic tale of a forgotten wedding anniversary, an anguished, guilty husband and a wife to whom he'd promised the same recording they'd bought on their honeymoon, long since broken—the record, not the promise or the marriage.

Osterweil finished and held his breath like a pianist holding down the keys long after the final chord has died into silence. Levine reached for the phone.

The address was in Brentwood Park. Bad news! Lots of money on these elegant, tree-guarded streets. A mere cash offer might not carry the day. Things became even more complex when he parked his car in the circular driveway and rang the bell.

"Hi." Beige blouse, tan slacks, and high-piled blonde hair. "I'm Jay," she said. "I seem to have gotten your recording."

He had not expected a woman; and such an hospitable woman. She invited him into the living room, sat him down next to the Steinway, gave him a Diet Coke, and listened to his Beethoven quest story. Which he prefaced by remarking: "Aren't you a little overly trusting?" It was Osterweil's way of expressing how weird he felt, in a stranger's home in the middle of the afternoon in a city that was still foreign to him, thunder rippling in the distant air.

"Trusting?"

"Well, I'm a strange man."

"You don't look very strange. What do you do?"

"I'm an English professor at UCLA."

"That's pretty safe. Besides, you come recommended."

"By a clerk I'd known for ten minutes."

"He's not a clerk—he's the boss. Besides, people looking for Beethoven are not usually looking for trouble. Tell me the story."

Feeling like a criminal, Osterweil repeated the wife/honeymoon/record story he'd told Levine at the Musical Gryphon. The young woman—she couldn't have been more than twenty-five—listened, first with her wide blue eyes open, then closing them towards the end of the recitation.

"I'll pay you double what you paid, if that's any help," Osterweil concluded. "You can see how—"

She stood up. Her knife-neat slacks were the opposite of Rowena's flowing skirts. A trim, authoritative figure, she went to the stereo unit against the wall and picked up a CD, apparently the famous performance itself.

"I won't sell it to you," she said. "I'll give it to you." She waved it at him.

"Oh?"

"On two conditions."

"Okay . . ."

"First, that you tell me the *real* reason you're carrying on like this about a goddam recording. Mr. Osterweil— did I get it right?" She made no pause for a reply. "You are not a crazy person, Mr. Osterweil. I wouldn't have let you in if you were. I can tell that about a person right off—you pick up that knack in L.A.; a necessary survival skill, like carrying a flare in the trunk of your car. So, if you drop this crap about your honeymoon and June and spoon and tell me why you're getting yourself all bent out of shape about a Beethoven sonata, late, early, or right on time, then I promise you I'll hand it over, on the spot."

She was breathing sort of hard, now; anger or other unnamed agitation, it was hard to tell which. To deflect this unexpected turn in the encounter, Osterweil could only think to say, "What's the second condition?"

"That all this has absolutely nothing to do *with Anne-Marie and that business in Oakland."* Long, heavy pause, then: "Because that was a hell of a long time ago and everything's changed for a lot of people since then."

Wow, Osterweil thought, what the hell am I into and how do I get out?

"Jay," he said. "Did I get *your* name right? J-A-Y?"

"Actually it's J-e-a-n-n-e. But they call me Jay."

"Well, Jay, it sounds to me as if I have one shot to get you to believe me. Because the story I told was made up for the guy at the record store—and then I was stuck with it. So, here goes."

And he pretty much began with the Stevens class and Rowena Ralph and flashbacked to his Thanatosis and even something about his divorce from Nina along with a brief coda about how nobody could make up *this* story, and said that he had never been to Oakland and knew no Anne-Marie. He told it as truthfully as he knew how and in some way it must have worked because she never said one more word, just handed him the recording and stood at the door open to the winds and roiling clouds, looking at him with reproachful, young, disbelieving eyes.

Osterweil dashed from his garage to the house and into the living room. It seemed a year since he'd decided that this music was to crown his entire mortal adventure. But it had just been a day—less, about three hours since dashing from his class into the car. The morning when he'd taken refuge in Emerson's wonderful phrase "glad to the brink of fear" was a lifetime ago. So much, he thought, for his miserable bookishness. Whatever had happened to someone named Anne-Marie in Oakland, it had happened in a life, not in a book. And it was still haunting Jay/Jeanne in some way he would now never know.

He headed for the living room to close the windows against the storm that felt imminent; the air was warm soup. But en route to the living room he saw the light blinking on his telephone answering machine.

There were two messages, both from his picnic friends. He listened to their voices as someone might who had come back from a long illness; a convalescent trip. The first message was from Al Stepner. This was Dr. Stepner the "scientist," Stepner the consoler of all mere mortals who may foolishly be concerned in the face of predictions of natural doom. "To all members of the Santa Monica Picnic Verein-Gangen—especially the Osterweil branch: do not be dismayed by reports of flood and fire. Flood no—fire, yes. But my experience is: lightning is that which one reads about having struck someone else. Can anyone listening to this message testify otherwise? Appear at the appointed time or be damned."

The second was less oracular but equally designed to make Osterweil feel friended. It was the sweetly Viennese-accented voice of Lorelei Kessler. "This is Lorelei and it just occurred to me that it might be the right time for you to bring someone to the party, tonight. A girl, no? Not essential, but maybe fun, yes? Bring an umbrella."

With the messages received and the windows secured, the weird rush he'd been feeling subsided.

Osterweil crashed.

Now that he was home again, he felt the pulsing of the old anxieties. He knew with absolute certainty that he must do two things: drop Rowena Ralph from the Stevens class and announce that he would not be at the picnic tonight. The skies were growing dark and he had not even begun making the shrimp salad, his specialty made with a curry like no one else's on the West Coast, which was to have been his contribution to the evening. Instead, once again, he envisioned his own obsequies, felt the absolute certainty of his death and heard a voice (Stepner's?) intone: ". . . a failed poet—no poems, a failed husband—no wife, and failed father—no children—an untenured teacher, an uncertain friend. . . . He knew no one named Anne-Marie and was never in Oakland. . . ." The first all-negative eulogy in history. There would follow a strange, hushed pause while the record was inserted.

God, it was awful, this moment before the playing of the Beethoven. He had the recording in his hand now; was he holding his own finish, the last variation on the theme of Osterweil in the world? It was Rowena, he decided, Rowena Ralph with her forcing of the issue—was she a Catholic, Protestant, or some member of a California sect, a believer in the Great All? She had been so crazed in her struggle with the Wallace Stevens poem, proudly declaiming:

> But in contentment I still feel
> The need of some imperishable bliss.

These were the lines of the woman the poet considers in the poem. Accent on the word "imperishable." That was Rowena's last insistence. But now he would call her up and read her the next lines.

Death is the mother of beauty . . .
. . . Although she strews the leaves
Of sure obliteration in our paths . . .

Osterweil longed to act with force and point; to leave someone, as Nina had left him; to drop a student from a class. . . . It was necessary once before you died, to approach gladness with the same indifferent strength with which it approached you.

He would call her and then he would tell her he was dropping her from the course, that anyone who could so misunderstand a major work by a major poet was— God, how would that sound when it came up at the Academic Council. He was already a long shot for promotion to full professor. Okay, he would ask her to withdraw from the course—to take an incomplete.

Why? she would ask, as if he had explained nothing. Why? And he would answer—because you tried to cure my Thanatosis with medicine that doesn't work? Because you let me win my death and now I'm stuck with it for the rest of my life. No, that's not quite fair. Because the skirts sliding between your legs promise only the heaven of moments that come before death—not instead of it.

The student phone directory was in the kitchen near the phone. It would be a difficult call.

"Rowena Ralph, please."

"Yes . . ."

"Rowena, this is Professor Osterweil."

"Hello."

"This is Professor Osterweil."

"Yes, I understand. I was just saying 'hello.' "

"I'm sorry. I wasn't sure you heard me."

"That seems to be a continuing problem with us, doesn't it?" She had jumped right in. He was impressed.

"That's why I'm calling."

A roll of thunder cracked. Osterweil jumped.

"Did you hear that?"

"Yes, I can hear you."

"I meant the thunder."

"Oh, it's raining over here in the Valley already. No thunder, though."

Osterweil fell into the long pause that followed.

"Listen, I have something important to tell you, Rowena."

It wasn't feeling right, Osterweil thought. Stall.

"By the way, do you know you remind me so much of Rowena in Ivanhoe. Down to your yellow braids."

"I've never read Walter Scott."

"Ah."

"I'm very much a modernist."

"Yes, I know. That's why you're doing Stevens."

"Or being done in by him." She laughed. "Though I do love him so." It felt as if they'd been chatting for years, for decades. This was not good. Osterweil summoned his tattered will. "Listen," he said. And astounded himself by saying, "Did you notice how I made a mistake and said 'the next clash' the other day, instead of 'class'?"

"How could I not? We *were* having clashes."

"Listen," he said again, "Listen . . ."

"Yes."

And astounded himself once more. He was going to do it!

"I'd like to invite you to a picnic tonight. Along the ocean in Santa Monica."

Her laugh was a yes but also a laugh. "The ocean in the rain. I'd love it," she said. "I should get credit for it—oceans and weather—very Wallace Stevens."

He was as relieved as if his original plan had worked.

"These are not academic people. They're close friends; a mixed group. This is an annual event. I don't mean to make it sound so important; it's just a picnic and there may be rain and lightning." He was bumbling so and yet she acted as if it was a sane conversation.

"You know, Professor Osterweil . . ." she began. He did not step forward to attack the first-name problem, yet. There would be time for that. "Since you've asked me to join you," she said softly as if prepared, "I want you to know I'm not dumb, I'm not hostile, and I'm not just out of a convent or anything. I know what Stevens is up to in 'Sunday Morning'—it's so beautiful the way he denies heaven in favor of an earth for mortals. *The heavenly fellowship of men that perish and of summer morn* . . ." Rowena Ralph's voice shook a little, he thought. It was hard to tell on the phone. "I know he's trying to make it—you're trying to make it all a kind of mournful comedy. . . . But sometimes I just mourn. . . ."

"Me too, Rowena," he actually said, surprising himself again. "Sometimes I mourn in advance." But she was not listening.

"I just mourn and I forget the universal comedy—sometimes right in the middle of your class—and then I'm left with all this dying, first my father and now my brother in Oakland. . . . That's why I struggled so much, so stupidly, like some religious fanatic . . . and . . . oh, never mind, the answer is yes, yes I'd love to picnic with you and your friends . . . yes . . . thank you . . ." Now she sounded a little weepy. Oakland again, Osterweil thought. Is Oakland the secret center of the universe?

"What shall I wear?" Rowena Ralph was saying.

The proper answer would obviously be slacks for sitting on the beach, or grass, or blankets or benches, especially given the menace of rain. Instead Osterweil said, "I loved that dress you wore in class today," and she said, "I'm still wearing it, so I'll just keep it on."

And Osterweil knew everything was changed between them, forever, from that moment. She would have to drop his class or he would have to marry her to avoid charges of sexual harassment, which at that moment was absolutely fine with him.

He turned the power on for the stereo. There was no way he could begin making the shrimp salad for tonight *before* playing the Beethoven. *While*, perhaps, but certainly not *before*. He had no recollection that either he or Rowena Ralph had said goodbye, yet they were no longer on the phone. And the instant he turned away from it towards the recording, the blackness returned, the threat of his own absence was somehow more intense. It was as if Rowena Ralph's voice on the phone had plugged him back into life and hanging up had broken the connection. He had actually told her about his "Thanatosis"— well, at least about his mourning in advance; though he had not confided it was *himself* he mourned for. There was a crackling of thunder outside, more distant now for being beyond closed windows; dreamlike for being in darkening daylight.

As he slipped the recording from its container he felt obliterated, as close to absent as you can be and still breathe. He recalled a line from a poem about death, it might even be called "Death." It was not Stevens but who? It didn't matter. Evening was on its way. No one could be an English professor at evening.

Most things won't happen.
This one will.

His mother had died, young, unachieved, full of personal regrets, strong and gentle; his father died older, full of years and irritable business plans, tough then weak. Both of them utterly New York. Their deaths had made it easier to come west with Nina. But strangely they were still dead, she was gone, and he was still floating about in L.A.

For a second Osterweil fell, spinning into the dark hole of nothing, left only with enough strength, and barely that, to pick up the CD. He slipped it into the cavity, which sucked it deeper into the dark for which the interior of the CD player was only an idea, a model, as if oncoming night outside his window was not model enough.

He stood there, in one hand the unread recipe for the Shrimp Salad Curry he was to create, without which, somehow, the night of the world could not proceed; the other hand open, half curled, where the recording had briefly rested before its journey into the underworld to rescue a song.

Gilels began the variations, gently stating the theme, three notes, two of them descending, repeated, gentle enough to allow Osterweil to move quietly into the kitchen, to start measuring out the necessary spices. Was Gilels still alive, he wondered, or was this the Russian pianist's posthumous song, as well? Then the adventures of the melody commenced. Twisted, developed beyond expectations, retarded, syncopated, extended, paused, rushed— not unlike the convoluted day Osterweil had just plunged through. As if to accompany the notes he poured oregano, then cinnamon—paused to allow the reality of a peeled shrimp to settle.

But the movement grew wild, leading to a high treble tracing of the melody; then it fell to a series of suspended chords which finally opened out into the broad, open-armed statement of the full theme. It swept Osterweil and his grief and fear before it, allowing for no argument, no holding back; some faint memory of the music's insistence on the heroism of gladness may have been why he'd chosen it in the first place.

The gladness of the morning invaded Osterweil again; a joy as overwhelming as the anxiety and gloom. With the expansive sounds at his back, and the pepper mill in his hands, he was glad—how weak the word sounded, detached from Emerson's wild snow-puddled experience, now that it had to become Osterweil's own gladness. He was glad to have lived . . . not just glad to be alive now and the very next moment—a gladness that filled his chest to bursting. Not just glad to be going to a picnic on the beach with the certainty that they would all be drenched in the wild savage rain that was blowing up. Glad for his own being . . . glad to be the kind of nervous, overly cautious man he was—a man who had thus missed out on a lot—whose one adventure had been to follow a lawyer-wife out to a strange land only to be abandoned by her to an untenured career and a serious case of Thanatosis.

But glad, too, to be the man who had invited Rowena Ralph, a young woman who had, astoundingly, never read *Ivanhoe*, had invited her to picnic with his friends instead of dropping her from the Stevens class. Though he had no idea how she would mix with the sharp-tongued ironies of their little group. What would she make of Lorelei, with her Schubert songs of moonlight and the sea, of French and his bitterness about the business success of others, of Stepner and his heavy-handed doctor's jokes, *Lightning is that which one reads about having struck someone else* . . . of Kessler—of—

Osterweil noticed that he was thinking of what *she* would make of *them*—not vice versa. Already, the intensity of the group was fading under the encroaching double shadow of Rowena and himself. Typically, Osterweil was rushing, in his imagination, towards a life the way he had been rushing in recent weeks towards a death. Equally unreliable, this business of envisioning lives or their absences.

Yet, under the spell of the Beethoven he'd struggled so hard to bring home, he allowed his gladness to spread to an imagined future in which he and his second wife, Rowena Ralph, read aloud together, fought, and read aloud to each other again, the two of them eternally, incorrigibly bookish and in conflict, forever. After, of course, a honeymoon in Provence where the July days would stretch so long that they could have dinner at an outdoor café clinging to the side of a tiny perched village at ten o'clock at night, still light, with flights of starlings swooping about their heads below a sky spattered with stars.

It was all so real to him, even the arguments. They would be about large matters—the nature of the Universe, what this or that poet meant, about understanding Wallace Stevens. *Death is the mother of beauty* . . . But it would come down to precise conflicts, too: should the children have a religious education? As he stirred and listened and planned Osterweil also knew that, like his death and the accompanying music, it might not happen at all the way he imagined. Rowena might be already married, engaged, a lesbian. She might have a fixation on much younger men, on much older men. But at that moment he was simply so glad to be in the presence of the possibilities that none of the uncertainties mattered.

Osterweil went into the living room, mixing bowl in hand, and turned up the volume of the music so that anyone in hell or heaven could hear it. He stirred his special salad and saw that the night had come, heavy with clouds, but as yet no rain. He turned the volume up even more and followed the Beethoven, noble in its steps, expansive in its song, and he was glad.

Glad to the brink of fear.

Wakefield

by

Nathaniel

Hawthorne

(a Story by Daniel Stern)

"THAT'S THE the strangest story I ever heard," Geneen said.

"That's how it struck me. Fascinating."

"Well, *strange* is what I said."

"He just walked away from his wife, away from his home," Burk said.

"And stayed around the corner, secretly, for over a year?"

"No, no, for almost *twenty* years."

"Yes," Geneen said. "That's the crazy thing of it." She was dabbing a kerchief at her cheeks where snow had melted. "Observing her, you said."

"Think of it." Burk was aware that he was talking faster than usual. "Watching her for almost twenty years. And it was supposed to be an ordinary business trip—two or three nights. Home by Friday, I think he said."

"*Supposed* to be. . . ?"

"Well, he invented a trip because he was going to play this little trick on his wife. He kissed her goodbye as she stood in the doorway . . ."

"Then went around the corner and took a room in a motel."

"But only for a night—he thought. He was improvising. It seems Hawthorne was clear about that."

"Watch out," Geneen said. A waiter had almost tripped on Burk's suitcase. "Better shove that under the table. Why didn't you check it?"

"This book with this story I wanted to show you is in there."

"This Winfield story."

" 'Wakefield.' "

"Sorry."

"I didn't have time to dig it out. As soon as they said there was a flight to Logan, I flew."

"I would think, after being trapped for seven hours."

"Nine."

"Poor Burko."

He leaned across the table and brushed his lips across a wet cheek.

"Aha," she said. "I was wondering when and if. When the surprise call to lunch came, well, I wondered . . ."

Burk never enjoyed her habit of saying "aha." Like her habit of occasionally not completing sentences, letting them float. He must be especially glad to see her tonight, because none of it bothered him.

"Well," Burk said. "That was not our finest goodbye scene. Cold stuff."

Apparently she wasn't ready to tackle that. She said, "Not as cold as Buffalo. Reuben called. He got nervous when he saw the blizzard on TV. I told him I'd spoken to you and that you were okay. I lied."

"How's the kid?"

"Tired of Putney. He wants to come home. He's straightened out nicely."

"I don't think just yet."

"He's all right there for now. But you—you look like a telephoto of yourself."

"A stewardess said it was the worst snowstorm in Buffalo in the whole decade. Stumbling on this wild and beautiful story may have saved my sanity."

"Beautiful?"

"Crazy but beautiful in a way I can't figure out yet. I'll read some of it to you. It's quite short. Anyway, it was an awful endless night."

"I think you mentioned something about this 'Wakefield' when you were finally able to get through. But you were pretty frantic by then."

"Having this story dropped in my lap felt like some weird act of destiny."

"Destiny?"

"You get a little crazy yourself, trapped in a freezing airport—"

"No heat?"

"It seemed to go off about halfway through and I couldn't get a straight answer from anybody about why or when it might come on again. Then in the ninth hour this guy leaves the book on the seat next to me. Open to this actual story."

"When we were first married you read a lot. You used to read to me—*Père* . . ."

"*Goriot*. And you read Dickens to me. *Bleak House.*"

"Long time."

"Consultants don't read. We scan for information. But this little—I don't know what you'd call it—anecdote—tale—it got to me."

Burk scrambled with his hands under the table. A zipper compartment yielded and he pulled out a gray-covered book. "Look," he said. "It's published by the University of Texas Press. I don't think I've seen a book published by a university press since New Haven."

She threw back her heavy gray cloth coat and a rich smell of wet wool came across the table. "You know," Geneen said, "I wasn't sure we'd ever sit across a table again." She was getting closer to the bone.

"Because of what I said? About the house in Wellfleet?"

"And the money . . ."

"Was I all that bad?"

"Or maybe what *I* said—I don't remember anybody's words anymore. It just wasn't a whole lot of fun."

"Well," Burk said, "I'm glad you were in the office when I called."

"Let's order first," she said. "I'm starved."

"How about a drink before lunch?"

"A drink drink? I can't remember when either of us—"

"Come on, Genny. You can fake your way through the rest of the afternoon."

"I'll have to close the office early, anyway."

"Right. This town stops cold after four inches of snow."

They had a table near the window, one floor up, so the snow slanted across the glass, changing shapes and distracting their gazes, hers already quickly shifting, oblique, driven by nerves.

"Are you going to have a strike?" Burk asked, still browsing the pages.

"Not if I can help it."

"Good. The last strike they had the union worked you so damned hard I never got to see you when I came home from various assorted airports. I think maybe that's why we had that fuss before I left for Buffalo."

"Aha," Geneen said. "The crisis is now only a fuss. Like when they downgrade a hurricane to just a tropical storm."

"I was feeling stale. I grabbed onto the summer house stuff as an excuse. Anyway maybe this can be a celebration lunch."

"Some secret stuff going down here?"

"Something hit me around four A.M."

"And that's the reason you had me break a lunch date with the president of the local to have lunch at the Ritz?"

"Spur of the moment. Right at the baggage claim it occurred to me—lunch with my wife; a surprise for both of us."

He ordered a margarita on the rocks, no salt. Burk could see her registering the unaccustomed tequila at midday. She would have something to say. He waited, braced. But what she said was, "How did the gig go?"

"I must have sold thirty heavy-duty systems. Since you ask."

"I'm glad you called. It's been a while since you raced home to share an idea."

"That damned little story jerked my head around. I don't feel stale anymore. I kept wanting to tell you about it."

"A white wine spritzer, for me, please," Geneen told the waiter. Then: "You always hate when I have little secrets or spring surprises. But you love them for yourself."

She was still on edge. He'd had the distractions of being

prisoner of a terrorist snowstorm and the discovery of "Wakefield." She'd had the time and space to brood.

"You look especially pretty," Burk told her, "with snowflakes on your eyelids."

"I was hoping you'd notice before they melted." He could see she'd needed a compliment, attention of some kind, to melt a smile onto her mouth. The careful way he'd placed it didn't seem to matter one bit.

The drinks came, and with the kind of excitement an author might have at reading a new work to his wife over a drink, Burk opened the book. He said, "Now mind you this is Chinese boxes, because it starts with a piece by this Argentine writer Borges—I don't know how to pronounce that—should it rhyme with gorgeous?"

"Sorry. I took German and you took French."

"Anyway, it's him telling about a story by Hawthorne which fascinated him."

"And now fascinates you," Geneen said, looking up at him with caution over her wineglass.

"Yes," he said and, relentless, read:

"Hawthorne had read in a newspaper, or pretended for literary reasons, that he had read, the case of an Englishman who left his wife without cause, took lodgings in the next street and there, without anyone's suspecting it, remained hidden for twenty years. During that long period he spent all his days across from his house or watched it from a corner, and many times he caught a glimpse of his wife. When they had given him up for dead, when his wife had been resigned to widowhood for a long time, the man opened the door of his house one day and walked in—

simply, as if he had been away only a few hours. (To the day of his death he was an exemplary husband.)"

Burk paused. Geneen was in the middle of a long, slow sip of wine. He could not read her reaction.

"Exemplary," she said. "Well . . ."

"The details are the strange stuff. It's an ordinary October evening and Wakefield is going to take the stagecoach—"

"Oh, I thought it took place today. I don't know why."

"No, it's London at the beginning of the nineteenth century. His wife doesn't ask the reason for the trip or where or anything. She's used to his little secrecies. Wakefield is wearing boots, a rain hat, and an overcoat; he carries an umbrella and a valise."

"Good old London," Geneen said. She sipped at her wine. Burk still could not read her reaction. London had been one of their favorites. She'd once said that they'd never made love badly in London. But by this time he couldn't stop; anyway by now he was speeding again. It reminded him of his Dexedrine days in college.

"It's not cut and dried. The author is as astonished as I was. Listen: *Wakefield—and this surprises me—does not yet know what will happen. . . . He goes out, closes the front door, then half opens it, and, for a moment, smiles."*

"He doesn't know that he's going to be playing this horrible joke on her—but he smiles?"

"He knows but he doesn't know. Years later Wakefield's wife will remember that last smile. She will imagine him in a coffin with the smile frozen on his face, or in paradise, in glory, smiling with cunning and tranquillity. Everyone will believe he has died but she will remember that smile and that perhaps she is not a widow."

The interior of the dining room was filling with the bluish Boston winter light of afternoon. There were only a few other couples who had toughed out the weather. The elegant dining room was a blur of white, tablecloths at empty tables, snow smearing the broad windows, and Burk felt the occasion full of the specialness he'd wanted. In spite of his aching exhaustion and his uncertainty about Geneen's response, he felt lucky.

"It seems that what he had in mind was to disturb or surprise his wife by staying away from home for a whole week."

"A practical joke?"

"Some joke. After he runs like a thief to rooms he's reserved in advance . . ."

"He's thought this out."

"Not so well. He's still improvising. When he gets to the hotel, terrified that somebody has seen him, he feels as if he's reached the end of a triumphant journey."

"He's one street away, you said."

"And soon he goes to bed." Burk read, *"Almost repentant, he stretches out his arms in the vast emptiness and says aloud: 'I will not sleep alone another night.'"*

"Ha," Geneen said.

"And in the morning he wakes up and asks himself what he's going to do now—then realizes he's going to find out what effect one week of being a widow has on his wife."

"Ass. One more drink and then food, okay?"

Geneen switched to a margarita. Burk noted the change.

She seemed to be letting go a little; beginning to be interested, less afraid of what might be coming.

"He goes out to spy on his own house from a distance—but out of habit he ends up almost at the door. He panics and beats it to the corner. From there he turns and looks back."

"You know," Geneen said. She leaned back on the banquette for the first time since sitting down. "This doesn't feel like a story from the last century."

"And here—he looks back at the house—and it seems different to him. Because he's already a different man, so says Mr. Borges."

Geneen removed the foolish-looking striped straw from her margarita and drank directly from the glass. "Well, of course," she said. "It's all going to be different for him from now on. He's stepped out of the loop."

"What?"

"The loop. Everybody's in the loop, one loop or another. Once you step out—you're out!"

Burk was delighted. Geneen smiled. He had forgotten how a smile on her face could take it from dark to brightness so quickly.

"It's nice, us talking like this," she said. "Unexpectedly. I was nervous at first."

"Because of the story?"

"And because it was so important for you to tell me about it right away, and that's keeping me nervous." She raised her glass in a mock toast. "I figured I'd give you and the story a little leeway. But I needed some help."

They clink glasses. Forgetting about his own drink, Burk tells her about Wakefield's adventure. How he actually buys a reddish wig as a disguise. How he worries that his absence has not upset his wife enough—won't go back until he's given her a good scare. Geneen remarks that he's more like a child running away from home than a husband—wasn't it Tom Sawyer who did something like that? she murmurs over the rim of her glass. But Burk presses on. "Wakefield keeps watching the house, and one day the druggist goes in and out, another day the doctor."

"Isn't *that* enough for him?"

"Well, he's afraid that if he comes back suddenly while she's sick—it'll be dangerous for her."

"You *believe* that?"

"It's what he believed."

"You believe *he* believed that?"

"I don't know. But these next two parts gave me the shivers. Listen: *Obsessed, he lets time pass; before he had thought, 'I shall return in a few days,' but now he thinks, 'in a few weeks.' And so ten years pass.*"

"My God," Geneen breathes. "I believe that."

"That blew me away," he says, "those five words—*and so ten years pass.*"

"Yes. I don't know why but I absolutely believe it could happen."

Burk continues, *"For a long time he has not known that his conduct is strange. With all the lukewarm affection of which his heart is capable, Wakefield continues to love his wife, while she is forgetting him."*

"Yes," Geneen says, "Yes, of course." She is all yeses, now. It is not a monologue he has brought back from his travels. The two of them are now, in some new way, putting this story together. She seems as taken by the tale as he is. He has no idea if it's the wine, the tequila, or Wakefield; if she was nervous before, she is all eagerness to go on, now.

"What was the second thing?"

But the waiter is at the table. They look at him for an instant as if he's from another planet, as he speaks of luncheon specials, of things baked and broiled and greens with vinaigrette. Burk takes charge and simple things are ordered, omelets and salads and a different wine.

"The second thing?" she prompts. She has finished her margarita and the words come nice and easy now.

"He actually meets his wife face to face."

And Burk tells how one Sunday morning the meeting happens by chance on a crowded London street. Wakefield is thin, now, he walks like a fugitive; his face, which was common before, is extraordinary now, because of his extraordinary conduct.

"Does he say what his wife looks like?"

"Yes, she's grown stout, carrying a prayer book; completely the placid, resigned widow."

"Ha. He sees her but does she see him?"

"Apparently they look into each other's eyes and are quickly separated by the crowd."

Geneen reaches across the table and takes the book from his hands. "Let me read this part for myself," she says. And reads: *Wakefield hurries to his lodgings, bolts the door, and throws himself on the bed, where he is seized by a fit of sobbing. For an instant he sees the miserable oddity of his life."* Geneen pauses, looks up at Burk and then, with sudden passion, *" 'Wakefield! Wakefield! You are mad!' he says to himself."*

Burk takes the book back. She yields it easily; this is a new game, like children reading and being read to at bedtime. The fresh wine arrives, white for her, red for Burk. And the hot plates bearing omelets and the cool ones with salads. Geneen moves the single red rose in a bud vase to an adjoining table. There must be nothing between them and the theme on which they are playing their variations. Burk and Geneen keep tossing Wakefield and his fate back and forth across the table. They eat and talk, like people not entirely familiar with each other, a couple on a date.

Geneen—"That was just one flash—one stunning moment. You can't keep up a masquerade like that, all the time thinking you're a madman."

Burk—"He's been repeating the words 'I shall soon go back' and doesn't realize he's been doing it for twenty years. Twenty years of solitude is an interlude to him, a parenthesis."

Geneen (dreamily)—"My goodness God . . ."

Burk—"Can you believe . . ."

They lean back at the same moment, the same cadence. They are playing at the game of Reading Wakefield as if it were an old family holiday habit the way they used to reread Dickens (her favorite) or Balzac (his favorite) with Reuben sitting on the floor between them. All that remains is to finish lunch and, over coffee, they can return Wakefield to his destination and get on towards theirs.

"What did he think was—?"

"I don't think all this was what you could call *thinking.*"

Geneen poured some more of the white for herself. She let her head loll against the brown banquette. "Remember once we gave a party and one of Reuben's teachers was there."

"The one that made a pass at you?"

"But before that he made a lot of literary small talk. He said Hawthorne vanished from the world for a long time. Just like—"

"We had a lot of parties in those days."

"I wasn't back to work yet."

"And I was in my restless phase," he said, remembering the childish dizziness of all the possibilities—of becoming the first professor of Artificial Intelligence at Yale, of making a zillion dollars in international import-export. "I was still having dreams of glory."

"International," Geneen said. "You wanted anything international."

"I spoke French. And I wasn't even thirty yet."

"And you liked airports—until last night you liked airports."

She pushed her wineglass carefully out of reach and said, "Actually, it's one of the the cruelest, ugliest stories I've ever heard. It's full of fascination and sympathy for this wild man and not one word of concern for his wife."

"Lots of words."

"But all from the outside—the way Wakefield felt about seeing her."

Burk spread his hands, open, helpless. "It's not so much *about* her. Every story can't be about everybody. You said it before—it's about stepping out of the loop. And remember," Burk's voice sounded odd in his own ears, desperate, as he read, *"With all the lukewarm affection of which his heart is capable, Wakefield continues to love his wife, while she is forgetting him."*

The coffee was so hot it startled Burk's tongue. But Geneen drank hers quickly and poured another cup.

"What do you expect? She thinks she's a widow. She's gone back to some kind of life, and he's turned into a ghost."

He tried a smile. "But wait for the end," Burk said. "Ghosts have a way of coming back."

"Is there any cream for the coffee?" she asked. "This stuff is too damned hot."

When the cream came it turned out to be milk but Geneen made do. The coffee might have been a mistake. Burk saw her coming down too fast. Her face looked pale.

"Burk," she said. "You didn't rush down here in this blizzard just to tell me about the most unforgettable character you ever read . . ."

He examined the menu closely and tried some desserts on for size.

"No," Geneen said. "I've known your tricks for eleven years, your little secrecies. No putting me off with sorbets and out-of-season raspberries. I agree it's an amazing story. Even to think up. Even if it never happened. That's not what I asked you."

"But apparently it did happen. Hawthorne read it in a newspaper."

"Maybe. And after seven hours cooped up and frozen, you can turn a simple story into a kind of hallucination

. . . one you have to rush to share with me—or to scare with me . . ."

"Nine hours," he said. "Those extra hours are vital."

"Okay, nine."

"Because in those two hours I made a decision."

Geneen's eyes narrowed. Burk was held by the look of her eyes: large and clearest blue. Narrowed meant trouble. The occasional migraine, the occasional flare of temper. This time she just narrowed and watched. In what he hoped was a light and reassuring tone, he said, "I found the silliest and most important solution to this riddle."

"Good. I hate riddles, I love answers."

"I want us to buy that summer house."

"Because of 'Wakefield.' "

"Because of 'Wakefield.' "

"That's not an answer."

"I was half dozing just before the heat came back on, frozen and full of fantastic thoughts, and suddenly I knew that Wakefield pulled his vanishing act because he lived in a big city, in London. He had no elsewhere to go to. Elsewhere is essential."

Geneen laughed. She had to put her cup down.

"So all that trouble could have been avoided by a trip to—where do the English go? We were there."

"The Cotswolds?"

"Don't you remember, we did a day trip? All those precious little cottages."

Burk was not so pleased. "Let's not make this too silly. I also thought, like me or like anybody, his troubles must have been ordinary. And the real ugliness starts when he tries to do something so extraordinary."

"What kind of troubles would you think?"

"The story doesn't say, but probably the usual. I mean, how long is anybody's list? Career disappointments . . ."

"No international triumphs. Was that what your Rome, Paris, London was for you? Your 'elsewhere'?"

"Maybe." Burk grinned. "And maybe his wife doesn't understand him."

"You mean she can't figure out computer lingo—prefers plain union shoptalk?"

"And kids. Don't forget they may have had troubled kids."

"Poor dear Reuben," Geneen murmured. "He's in better shape, now, than we are. Listen, it's wonderful about Wellfleet. I hope the house is still there. But you're missing one simple point. For some reason he didn't feel important enough, alive! Who does! But 'dead'—"

She leaned across the table and kissed him on the mouth. He had lately forgotten how pleasantly soft that mouth could be.

"Well," Burk said.

"I don't believe any of this," Geneen said. "But it doesn't matter. You can have your little secrecies."

"Thanks."

"You know what I think? I think you wanted a way to melt that icy goodbye scene. A way to come back. 'Wakefield' was as good a way as any."

"That's pretty complicated." Burk shook his head in irony and admiration and gazed at his wife; she was gathering strands of clothing, the loose end of a belt, the untucked corner of her silk scarf. She had it all together, now; had been off balance and was back on. Burk was a practiced Geneen-watcher. You could do that without moving to the next street and spying. You could spy on your wife across a luncheon table. Any married man knew that. He examined the shapely, high-cheekboned drama of her face and remembered how many moments of pleasure they'd managed to give each other. Those moments were softly pleasant but vague in shape. The bad moments were precise, vivid; easy to call up in all their awful detail.

"I said your secrecies were little," she said and shook her hair out. "I didn't say they were simple. I'd better go. I've still got to close the place up. Are we playing doubles tomorrow with Bonnie and Jack?"

Burk picked up the forgotten book. "Eight o' clock. But we have to get this poor son of a bitch home, first?"

"I forgot."

"He *does* go home."

"All right," Geneen said.

She settles back in repose; a pretty woman, almost forty, finishing an unexpected lunch with her husband. Together they watch Wakefield taking his usual walk towards the home he still thinks of as his.

It is an afternoon like the thousands of previous afternoons in which he has spied on his own house; a gusty autumn night, swept with swift, sudden showers of cold rain. He sees that they have lighted the fire in the second-floor bedroom; grotesquely the flames project his wife's shadow on the ceiling. At this instant a rough pelting of rain chances to fall and the autumn wind drives the wet into Wakefield's face. He thinks—shall he stand wet and shivering, outside like this, when his own hearth has a good fire to warm him?

No! Wakefield is no such fool. He walks up the steps—heavily; twenty years have stiffened his legs since he came down those steps, though he seems not to notice. The door opens. As he goes in the last we see of him is the same crafty little smile of twenty years ago, ghostlike, on his lips.

Geneen's office was just around the corner from the Ritz, on Arlington Street; she toughed it out, collar up, turning in the whirling white to blow a kiss at him. He was standing in front of the hotel, his suitcase at his feet, waiting his turn for a taxi that would take him home.

A whip of windy wet snow flew at his face. Burk's eyes teared. He could feel the apple-redness of his cheeks flaming. Finally, fatigue slumped his shoulders and pressed into his bones; the artificial high of the last few hours was gone.

"Elsewhere," Burk said aloud. "That was real dumb. That's all there is."

"Excuse me, sir?" The doorman moved towards him.

"No, nothing." Burk waved him off.

Burk picked up his bag and moved one step up in the taxi line. The doorman, the God of Weather and Transportation, an immense white-speckled figure in gold braid, nodded. Burk nodded back. There were two men and a woman in front him, also waiting. One man was short, elegant, holding silver-rimmed eyeglasses in his hand, as if they were no use in the snow; the other one was sitting patiently on his expensive-looking piece of luggage; the woman was tall, with an evasive, shy gaze. The gradual dark of the winter evening was pushing the afternoon to an early end. A kind of blue-black banality covered them all, Burk thought. They and their journeys seemed ordinary; nothing special; people on the brink of nothing more than a slow cab ride in a snowstorm.

How was it possible that he had never known about all this, before? Or did everybody find out about the "Wakefield" moment sooner or later—and this was just his time? And why had nobody, not the Argentinian writer, not Hawthorne, not Geneen—why had nobody considered what Wakefield said to his wife after his return, or what she might say to him?

Wakefield, you are mad, Burk thought, and his smile felt different, twisted, not his own, resting on his wet mouth.

He was next in line, now. A windsmash of snow struck him on the mouth, ugly with wet chill. He dropped his suitcase to the ground. The doorman came up to him, squinting through the fall of snow. "Cab, sir? You're next." Burk scrounged for a couple of crumpled dollars and shoved them at the man.

"Not yet, thanks," Burk said. He wrapped his scarf around his face. "Let's see if the weather turns. I'll wait awhile."

Bartleby
the Scrivener
by
Herman
Melville

(a Story by Daniel Stern)

I'M an agent, and among that special breed I am known as a cautious man.

I don't say yes, I don't say no. For the most part I say, "How about this arrangement?" or "How about that deal?" Note the question mark! Nothing is good or bad, of itself, in my universe. It either works or it falls apart. There is nothing of intrinsic value, although I have my own sense of ideal matters. What I deal with every day, however, is the precise opposite of ideal; it is called "material." Novels, screenplays, short stories, plays, outlines, ideas; it's all material. And in this working world it is a given that the nature of "material" is ephemeral. The treatment is everything.

This sometimes leads to personal problems, as when an intelligent, well-educated woman I knew fled this town after working too long on a treatment for *The Magic Mountain*, because, as she said, "I got tired of hearing Thomas Mann referred to as 'the property' "; left just when I was about to tell her I loved her. Just as well! I never quite knew how to explain her sudden defection to my partners, Alvin Rosen and Roland Ross. Alvin was too young and Harvard Business School to understand and Roland was too middle-aged and Hollywood-hardened. I told them she couldn't "lick" the love angle and then everybody understood.

But this story is not about my partners or me. We are here to talk about Roy Graubart, the king of Hollywood scriveners, a man who fell from grace even though he never quite rose to it. I use his own archaic term "scrivener" as an honorific for hack writers—my grandmother would have said "scribbler." I say "scrivener" the better to memorialize Graubart's passion for a certain tale of an earlier time. Graubart, himself, was certainly a scrivener circa 1980; his specialty was sequels at short notice. "I 'take in' writing," he would say at parties. He took great pleasure in positioning himself at the bottom of the Hollywood heap.

I said I was a cautious man but I have my enthusiasms. You might think, judging by the mention of Thomas Mann, that I had an especially "literary" clientele. Not so—you take what comes along if you think it will sell. Every now and then something comes your way whose special quality races your pulses; but by the time the system has gotten finished with it the special quality is gone and the pulse beat is sure to be back to normal. *The Magic Mountain* never got made—probably for the best.

But my personal background and taste are second-generation literary and European. It's what brought Roy Graubart to me, as a client. At a party he asked about my accent. And it turned out he'd heard of my mother, a screenwriter, a member of the group who fled the European terror of the Second World War for the sweet sunny safety of Los Angeles. Lion Feuchtwanger; Heinrich Mann and his more famous brother, Thomas; that crowd. My mother played in a regular mixed doubles game with Arnold Schoenberg, Salka Viertel, and Heinrich Mann. I was born in Vienna but raised in Los Angeles. At our first meeting Graubart told me all about the amazing courage of my parents' generation of refugees.

"If you knew how I idolize them. Everybody who acted with such courage over there with Hitler clamping down all over Europe."

I thought of the crazy parties of my childhood—the vodka and wild reminiscences of narrow escapes; of bribed border guards who kept their bribes and failed to deliver freedom. Among the dark mines of these memories there gleamed an occasional gold nugget of courage, of sacrifice; my Uncle Hersh, dead at twenty-six, who told the SS to go to hell. Instead of going themselves, they sent him on ahead.

"Do you think they all acted with such courage?"

"It doesn't matter," Graubart said. "Because I know I would have been a coward."

"How do you know?" I asked.

Graubart smiled. "Listen," he said. "One little arm twist and I would have turned in my best friends. I just know."

One got the idea that he'd thought about this subject for a long time. It gave his statement a weird kind of authority.

"Besides," he said, "those were enchanted days out here—Scott Fitzgerald living at the Garden of Allah, Salka Viertel having her literary salon in Westwood."

"It was in Brentwood," I said. "And you've mixed up two eras. Salka continued on into the fifties, Fitzgerald died in 1941."

Roy Graubart waved an impatient hand. "You know what I mean," he said. Small details such as the precise timing of a a figure or an era could not deter Graubart. In the intimate privacy of his soul he was after a sentimental ideal; his daily life might be all compromise and cowardice, but that, as he once said to me, was "only life," by which he meant only money. The rest was the way in which you imagined yourself—decided who you were.

Graubart was a "contract" writer; perhaps the last one around. He had never written an original in his life. Yet he had an enviable track record of employment. He'd worked at just about every studio, television network, and production company.

"They like me because I'm the last whore in town," he said. "Everybody else has gone straight—writing originals or buying properties and adapting them. I'm the last writer totally for sale or rent. No half-finished novel in the drawer, no short stories in *The New Yorker*, not even an act of a play-in-progress. The Compleat Hack. A weary but ever-ready Scheherazade, available to spin any tale that's needed—for a price. I was working on *Godfather III* nine years ago even though they were just going through the motions. Nobody, including Paramount, really wanted to make it. Finally, they took me off it because Puzo wanted to do it himself." There was a weird perverse pride in Graubart. Others had dreams of glory. He specialized in dreams of failure—failure of nerve, of courage, of independence.

In connection with this, he had read every memoir of the Holocaust, every scholarly book: he was the only screenwriter whose shelves bulged with names like Davidowicz, Ringelblum, Hilberg, and Wiesel. It was all as if to prove to himself, in case after case, how little courage he would have displayed under extreme pressure, compared to those who went through the war and the special horrors visited on Jews. All to prove that if put to the test, he would have been a sheep not a ram.

I was not looking for new clients. My partners and I had an informal agreement that I would retire on or about my sixty-fifth birthday. It had seemed like a bright idea, three years earlier when we discussed it. Lately, some of the brightness had dimmed. Maybe that's why I took Graubart on; sending a signal to my partners, to the production companies—most of all to myself—that I was still in action. And, as if to underscore this, I proceeded to get him a very classy development deal for a film of John Hersey's book *The Wall*—about the Warsaw Ghetto uprising. It turned out to be a disastrous idea. He gave up in the middle.

"You know why I couldn't handle it?" Graubart said. We were having lunch at Musso Frank's, a scrungy restaurant on Hollywood Boulevard. Roy loved it because of its association with famous dead screenwriters. The man lived on a diet of mixed nostalgias. It was part of what fascinated me about him. But the food was awful. I ordered chicken soup.

"I'll have the Herman Mankiewicz on Rye," Graubart told the waiter. He turned his attention to explaining the unthinkable—why he'd backed out of a deal to adapt a best-selling book; a deal I'd set up with great care and some luck.

"I couldn't handle it," he said. "Because I couldn't get inside those people."

"Which people?"

"The ones who took up the guns. The ones who finally said no."

"Why not?"

"Because every time I tried to feel what gave them the courage not to give in—I drew a blank. Zip. Zilch. In the Warsaw Ghetto I would have given up. If they handed me a gun I would have buried it and then hidden out for as long as I could in some cellar until I starved or they found me or the war ended."

I told him about my Uncle Hersh. Probably a mistake, reinforcing his separation of heroes from cowards.

"Tell me, Roy," I said. "Have you never done anything you'd call courageous?"

He thought for a long pause. Then he shook his head in the negative, seriously, slowly.

"What do I tell Krauss?" Lew Krauss was the current head of production at Columbia.

"The truth."

"He won't understand."

"Tell him that I couldn't get a handle on Greenspan, on Lestermann—the guys who grabbed machine guns and raced out to the streets, at the end, in spite of the fact that they were racing to absolute, certain death." He devoured his sandwich, ferociously. "Tell him I understand Lejkin much better."

"Who was Lejkin?"

"The head of the Jewish Police. He helped the Germans do their job because it gave him a longer lease on his own life. Now there's a character I can identify with."

Instead of getting Roy out of his Columbia deal, or telling Krauss any of Roy's personal reactions to the material, I convinced Graubart to team up with a co-writer, another client of mine, Anne-Marie Klein.

Anne-Marie was an old-timer—one of my little agency's main meal tickets. You've seen her films: the giant remake of Jean Renoir's *Grand Illusion,* the adaptation of Saul Bellow's *Henderson the Rain King.* Anne-Marie had an amazing knack for convincing hard-nosed film executives that they should do aesthetically daring projects. She was known as a class act yet she kept working. It was her elegant Viennese accent, she insisted with heavy-handed Mittel-European humor. She was five years old when she arrived in Los Angeles; her family had sweated out the war in Switzerland. Forty-five years later she still held on to her Schlagzammen thick diction. Anne-Marie had a routine explanation for it.

"When they run out of summer pictures by Spielberg and Christmas pictures by Lucas, when they need a release for grown-ups in February, they come to me because I talk like their parents, or their parents' friends. It's my secret for success," she said.

She had another secret these days; she was dying of cancer. I was the only one she told. It was the Hollywood ethos: when you get work you tell your friends and family; when you're mortally ill you tell your agent. Prim, coolly stylish, she'd never married and I'd never known her to entertain a romantic life. Some jokester at Universal nicknamed her the Hun-Nun, and it stuck. Three years earlier, I had arranged a four-picture deal for her at Warners and I was now eager to see her go as far as she could with it. Like everyone I knew who made a lot of money, she needed a lot. And, of course, endings of lives were much more expensive than beginnings.

Everyone except Anne-Marie thought I was crazy. She

was amused. "He calls himself a whore and they call me the nun. The whore and the nun, we make a fine team."

I actually was able to rewrite the contract so that if either one died or could not fulfill services for any reason, the surviving member would inherit all the rights and obligations of the deal. It wasn't an easy sale. After all, this was not Ben Hecht and Charles MacArthur I was selling—but I was desperate, relentless, and they gave it to me. That way I figured I was helping Anne-Marie and Roy. And it assuaged my uneasy sense that I was trapping Graubart into a partnership with a dying screenwriter.

They finished *The Wall* to Krauss's apparent satisfaction and it was shelved until the studio could find the right director. They were halfway through the next picture, Melville's "Benito Cereno" moved up to modern times, when it became clear that Anne-Marie would not be able to finish. She called me to come to her house in Santa Monica. There, in the living room filled with more books than I've ever seen in one room in Hollywood, except the public library, she told me.

"About two or three weeks, Dr. Steuben says. It's the pancreas now."

"I'm sorry, Anne-Marie."

"He says I could fight on longer; there's a fellow doing some experimental chemo at a clinic in Albuquerque, but all for the sake of a few more difficult weeks, maybe months. I told him no."

She poured me some thick espresso she had made but she had trouble holding the pot, as quiet about her courage as Graubart was noisy about his presumed lack of it.

"This will be bad for poor Roy," she said. "I've quite enjoyed working with him. His instincts are wonderfully dreadful. As soon as we started on 'Benito Cereno' he told me that Robert Lowell had done a play adaptation of it, years ago, and that we could steal a lot of it and save ourselves time and money. I told him no. The whore and the nun." She smiled, white-faced, tired.

"We were lovers for a few months, at first," she said. "I didn't know if you knew."

That Viennese style of sophistication: erotic confession en route to death. God! I just shook my head.

"It's going to make it hard for him. He's much younger than I am."

"Do you mind if I just worry about you?"

"Yes," she said. "I do. Let's both worry about Roy. It'll make it easier all around. By the way, I'm leaving you a lot of my books. I don't know many people who would enjoy them as much. Do you have room?"

"I'll make room."

I realized how long I'd known her and how little I knew about her—why did she never wear perfume, where did she go to college, had she ever almost married, things like that. Graubart told you everything in that New York/Los Angeles style—analyst, names and sexual feelings of divorced or separated wives, professional frustrations—all at the first dinner party or lunch.

She told him before I could. He was devastated. For the next three weeks—the doctor's predictions proved accurate—he spent most of every day and night at her bedside. I gather he read to her most of the time. Even when she began drifting into a deeper and deeper sleep.

But while she was still alert, in the early days, he discovered the story that set him on fire: "Bartleby the Scrivener" by Herman Melville. He called me the next morning and asked me to have a drink with him. He couldn't make lunch, but the changing of the nurses was about 6:00 P.M. Could I meet him for a drink at Ivy at the Shore in Santa Monica?

There was a warm rain, but it felt bitter; January in L.A. That morning Rosen and Ross, my partners in the agency, had asked me if I was going to make good on my promise to retire on my sixty-fifth birthday, which was coming up in March. Plans had to be made; younger people recruited, office space reevaluated, clients notified. Frankly, I'd forgotten that I'd had any such fantasy—spring in the south of France, summers in East Hampton, fall in New York, winter in Barbados. The arranged life. No more deals and counterdeals. I might barely have enough money to swing it. If my wife had been alive, if we had had children, it might have been different. But each time the idea crossed my mind, my stomach failed, my breath shortened. And when the subject was raised at the morning meeting my mood grew black.

But if I was feeling grim, Roy was lively. In spite of his deathwatch duties, the discovery of the "Bartleby" story had filled him with energy. I was used to this phenomenon—screenwriters calling me all charged up because they'd discovered some story they thought would make a great movie property. This excitement seemed more complex.

"I was browsing through that fantastic library of hers and I came across 'Bartleby' and read it aloud to her—she knew it, of course."

"Yes," I said. "Everyone knows those famous five words. *I would prefer not to.*"

"No," Graubart said, "not everybody. I never read it. And it's not just extraordinary—it's amazing!"

"All right, amazing. It's been years. I think I read it in college. It's a mystifying piece."

Roy proceeded to sing the song of the bleak, ghostly scrivener at a law firm who is hired to copy texts and, one day, when requested to verify a text says, "I would prefer not to." Then when asked to copy a text he repeats, "I would prefer not to."And from that time on he simply stares moodily ahead or out of the window and will perform no task he's asked to perform.

"Okay," Graubart said. "That's startling enough. But in a certain way it's as much about his poor boss—"

"Poor boss?"

"The man doesn't know what to do. He's a responsible lawyer, a businessman—it's called 'A Story of Wall Street,' by the way. Anyway, he becomes obsessed by this skinny crackpot of a man who simply refuses to go along with the ordinary demands of the world. The boss—they don't give him a name—"

"They?" It occurred to me that Graubart was treating this nineteenth-century classic as if it were a film treatment written by multiple hands. My mood improved. Watching Roy being Roy always cheered me up.

"Melville, I meant," he said, impatient to get on with his pitch. "Anyway the boss takes it and takes it—the other employees all laughing like crazy—and finally he *fires* him, Bartleby. And what do you think Bartleby says—"

I smiled; my first of the day. " 'I would prefer not to.' "

"Right! *He refuses to be fired.*" He grinned like a kid. "Imagine! But that's not the end. It's just the beginning." Graubart glanced at his watch. "I'll have one more martini," he said, "She's probably still sleeping, but if she wakes up I want to be there."

I ordered another for each of us and listened. There are two things agents learn to do early in the game: listen and pitch. Of course, out here everything you listen to is a pitch. But, for this moment I suspend my normal defenses and follow Roy's new friend, Bartleby, as he proceeds to live in the office, staying behind his screen, after being fired. Like a ghost who has not yet died, he haunts the chambers, a living denial of the managing lawyer's authority, perplexing visitors and casting a general gloom over the premises.

The narrator is driven to the edge of his nerves and tells Bartleby he must quit the offices, only to be met by *I would prefer not to.*

Graubart drained the last of his martini. "And feature this," he said. "Finally, the man says to him something like, Bartleby, either you do something, or something will be done to you. But even that doesn't work. Then, maybe the first time, ever, in fiction or in life, a boss, faced with an employee who refuses to leave, doesn't call the police and have him thrown out but instead *he actually wraps up his business and he's the one who moves,* just to get away from Bartleby. Leaving Bartleby in the same place."

He stood up. "I've got to run. The changing of the nurses' guard."

I asked, "Was there any special reason you had to tell me all this, now?"

He read my mind and said, "It wasn't really a pitch—but there's something important there. Got to get back now. I'll call you in a few days."

At the doorway he turned back. "I don't think I ever thanked you for putting me together with Anne-Marie. It's the best thing that ever happened to me."

"Even the way—things have turned out."

He nodded. "Do you know how to say 'I would prefer not to' in German? *"Ich ziehe es vor das nicht zu tun."*

"Yes," I said, fumbling for my credit card. "That's a rather formal way to say it. How do you know—?"

"When I read 'Bartleby' to Anne-Marie that's what she murmured after I finished. I asked her to repeat it until I had it memorized."

That night, before falling asleep, I drifted into a Valium reverie in which I became aware of the rare resonance of the phrase "I would prefer not to." It was, after all, what Anne-Marie had said, in effect, to the doctor when he offered to go on trying to save her life. And what would I say if my partners of thirty years, the eternal kid, Alvin Rosen, and the eternal judging father, Roland Ross—two men who were good colleagues but never quite friends—what would I say if they insisted on my honoring my commitment to retire? Too many endings, I thought. Only Graubart, with his raw scrivener's energy, seemed to have something up his sleeve, to be coming up with some fresh beginning.

The funeral was a modest, dignified event—lots of people who'd worked with Anne-Marie over the years; most of the eulogies and comments were devoted to the extraordinary courage of choosing her own way, in film projects and in how to die. It was a service you could hear only in L.A.

The next day Roy and I met for lunch at Chasen's. Many years ago he'd had dinner there with Bogart and Bacall; he was twenty-two and dating a girl who knew them. Time had moved past Chasen's. Electronics companies had their convention dinners there, now. But for Graubart it was still the Chasen's of old Hollywood; a mixture of lies and legend, all compounded of enchantment.

"I've got a tremendous idea for the next project," he said.

"Don't tell me," I said. I'd seen it coming.

Graubart grinned. "Right, it's 'Bartleby'—only brought up to the present. Well, not exactly the present. Germany in 1938."

"Oh, my God," I said.

"No, please—don't give up on me. Read the original material again. And then I'll tell you what I want to do."

"The studio will never go for it."

Graubart came out from behind the enormous menu. "I've read our contract. You're a genius. You arranged a deal in which I've got the right to choose the next picture, just as if we were still a working team."

"Contracts are only as good as the power behind them."

"And our power was buried yesterday, is that it?"

"Something like that."

"Read the story again. They say *The Treasure of the Sierra Madre* was planned at one of these tables. I'm not sure if it was this room, exactly. . . ."

Over coffee he said, "You know she changed everything for me."

Embarrassed, I said, "She told me you two were . . ."

"I didn't mean that. But even there she showed me you didn't have to choose between Tristan and Isolde or a dumb one-night stand. Love and sex isn't as black and white as it is in the movies."

I thought, the famous Viennese sophistication applied to an encounter between the nun and the whore.

He told me, "You should have seen who came to see her—in the industry, I mean."

"I can imagine. She was *sui generis*."

"What's that?"

"One of a kind."

"And how. What I really meant about her changing everything for me was about the writing, too. You know I don't have any illusions about what I do—but now—"

He was suddenly silent. When I pushed it, he told me to read "Bartleby" and we would meet at my office the next day.

That night I tried to sleep but I kept growing more and

more alert. Finally, I reached for "Bartleby" and began to read.

It was a meandering narrative until I got to Bartleby's arrival.

In answer to my advertisement, a motionless young man one morning stood upon my office threshold, the door being open, for it was summer. I can see that figure now—pallidly neat, pitiably respectable, incurably forlorn! It was Bartleby.

I registered with professional speed the four terms in that sentence which defined our "hero": motionless, pallid, pitiable, and forlorn. Normally, that would have been the end of the reading. But Graubart had reminded me of the bare bones and the strange dark mood infected me as I read. I read the thirty-one pages in about an hour—in the time I would usually polish off four times that number, for professional purposes. It wasn't that so much happened in the story. It was that almost nothing happened!

I followed the nameless narrator as he hired Bartleby, put him right near him so he could be helpful "in case any trifling thing was to be done" . . . followed Bartleby's progress from doing an extraordinary amount of writing . . . *As if long famishing for something to copy, he seemed to gorge himself on my documents . . . copying by sunlight and by candlelight. . . . I should have been quite delighted by his application, had he been cheerfully industrious. But he wrote on, silently, palely, mechanically.*

On the third day, Bartleby is asked by his employer to verify some copy. And it is then that he speaks the famous five words *I would prefer not to.*

From that moment on the scrivener's mysterious stubbornness takes over the tale; takes over the nameless narrator's whole life. Bartleby "prefers not to" do anything required of him, finally, not even scrivener's work—copying; not even leaving the premises to go home—he appears not to have one; and, finally, even after he is fired, he "prefers not to" leave the office.

At last the narrator quits the premises and moves elsewhere, rather than evict Bartleby forcibly. The next tenant has no such compunction—and Bartleby ends up in prison, refusing even enough food to stay alive. He dies in front of the poor, devastated lawyer who had first hired and then fled him.

I put the book down on the empty pillow next to mine. What was it that troubled me so about the story? It wasn't the kind of spiritually exciting temptation to civil disobedience that was thrilling Graubart, after decades of saying "Yes, I would prefer whatever you prefer, sir." No, it was much worse than that. It was the awful caution of the employer in the face of this astonishing wraith who was taking over his life. The caution of those who were so afraid of the dark side of life—

I remembered my wife, poor Helena, turning on me towards the end of our time together, with one word as weapon: cautious; the word I had always used to describe myself—but always with an overtone of self-approval. Caution, she said, was my word. The truth was, I was afraid of life. I had made her postpone having children, endlessly. My refugee panic, she said, masquerading as caution and care.

We would pass a playground and Helena would pick

out one particularly beautiful little girl or boy and say, "There, that one—that could have been ours. That boy— he sort of looks like you, actually."

It was eight years before we agreed to divorce. In those eight years she had two illnesses which made it impossible for her ever to have a child. The last illness made everything impossible, even life.

The book and the empty pillow next to mine were both cool or my face was hot. When I woke up, "Bartleby" was my pillow.

If I didn't know Roy better I'd have thought he was on a cocaine high at lunch. He had picked Citrus, very spare and Nouveau elegant. No history and very small portions. This was a new Roy.

"Did you read it?"

"Yes."

"Okay, now forget it. I mean forget everything you thought about it. We're in Warsaw—circa 1939."

"Roy, Roy—*The Wall*'s all done."

"Okay, forget Warsaw. Any small town in Eastern Europe. Bartleby's name is Klein. And he's the last Jew in the Judenrat. One leader they killed, one committed suicide—and Klein is left."

"My God—you want to take on that whole Hannah Arendt business? In a movie?"

"Well, yes and no. I mean—what do you think might have happened if somebody said, 'No, do your own dirty work. I'm a Jew and I'm not going to decide which Jews go first.' And they say: 'You make a selection—otherwise we'll kill them all.' "

I leaned back and stared at Graubart in a sort of weird admiration.

"Don't tell me," I said. "He, this Klein, says to them: 'I would prefer not to.' "

Roy's round face beamed. "You got it. And he says it again and again—each time they up the ante, just like in 'Bartleby.' He should be a kind of morose oddball like Bartleby. And the boss—the man who hired him and gets trapped by his resistance—becomes this SS colonel who likes Klein. In fact he sort of likes Jews. It's just that his job is to get the job done. And for that he needs help."

Our Perriers arrived and I wished mine had a sting of alcohol. This was not going to be easy.

I said, "My father liked to remark on how much help the SS had all over Europe. He meant the Poles, the Rumanians, the Ukrainians. He never mentioned the Judenrat."

"I've read stuff," Roy said carefully, "about how in the few places where somebody actually refused to go along with the system, the numbers say that the Jews did as well or better."

Graubart the scholar—all those fat books by Davido-wicz, by Hilberg. We ordered and I tried to touch a lighter note, while thinking what to do about this. I said, "Is this the right project for the famous whore?"

"I got the idea from the nun."

"This is Anne-Marie's idea?"

"No. It was hearing her say those words in German."

"People regress when they're dying. Childhood language comes back, sometimes. I've heard about it."

"Come on, you're weaving all around me. I'm hot on this one."

"I thought you couldn't get inside courage. Alien territory to you. You threw in the towel on a nice deal because of that."

He practically danced on the table. "Yes. But using Bartleby, this crazy, dark figure slowly drawing the net around himself so tightly that finally there was nothing inside except what he didn't 'prefer.' There's something so terrific about the idea of simply deciding to be exactly what you—you prefer—against everything people expect; Wall Street, the Nazis—that's the everyday world, money, power. But what about people who are asked to do things like the Judenrat. To pick out your own people to die, in the right order, so everyone won't be killed all at once. Something insane masquerading as sane . . . taking it all the way to some deep, absolutely irrational decision to be who you are—and that's all! As if other people—even the SS—not only had no power—it wasn't so much that—but that other people just didn't finally matter as much as what you prefer."

We continued sparring over something with raspberry vinaigrette and kiwi, arranged on the plate like Paul Klee being playful with food. It occurred to me that I had no other client quite like Graubart; that I had no clear idea of what my relationship to him was. It was certainly not the typical agent-client connection.

I had no self-styled "whores" in my stable; I was not a pimp. But for Roy, of all people, I had bent rules, forced

Krauss into rewriting a contract that would probably not hold up if ever challenged in court, and I'd made an unlikely match with Anne-Marie.

He barreled on about the big scene in which Klein is finally taken to the SS headquarters, where, like Bartleby, he starves himself to death, simultaneously frustrating and defeating the SS by his passive resistance. And half listening, I realized that on the level of dreams, fantasies, and regrets Roy might be one of those children of lost opportunity Helena used to point out to me, with her special irony, as we passed schoolyards, one of those children we'd never had, noisily playing in the unchangeable past.

After all, children were the ones with the wild ideas, the ones who had to be protected against the cold, uninterested universe. Children were the ones who kept trying to stretch the boundaries while the parents, dulled with the wisdom of experience, said: "They'll never go for this; this one will fail and you'll feel awful; listen to me." And then when the child refused to listen, the parents said, "Let me handle it. I'll protect you; I'll pay the bills; I'll pick up the pieces . . ."

It was good to feel this; as if it settled something with poor Helena. With this put to rest, my usually lively appetite returned and I decided that I would follow Roy in his madness, as far as I could. "Okay," I said, "What we have to hope is that somebody says yes without reading the original material. But we'll need a treatment."

He smiled roundly and handed me an envelope. "Read it and weep," he said.

•

It was the best thing he'd ever done; as close to an "original" as he could manage. There was a bite to it; and the story line worked. I told him this on the phone; he was happy but calm; he knew he was on to something good. What I didn't tell him was that the times were wrong, that nobody wanted World War Two stories just then and certainly nobody wanted something so heavyweight in aspiration from Roy Graubart. In this town you are what you've been. It takes an earthquake to change your slot in Hollywood's imagination. If you tried Sly Stallone playing Lear it would have to be comedy; and it would damage him forever.

In spite of all this I threw myself into the job of selling Graubart's "Bartleby" with a fresh energy. Sitting in a traffic jam on Mulholland, I thought of how many times I'd sat in that same hell of boredom and fumes, hiding from the heat or the rain or the smog behind my air conditioning, a script on the seat next to me, on my way to or from a pitch; and sitting there I had a glimmer of another truth. I realized I did not want to say goodbye to all this. Not just yet.

When I got to Krauss's office, Roy was waiting for me, and I surprised him and myself. I pitched the hell out of this lost cause. It was probably my unusually high energy, my lack of caution, that got Krauss and his coterie to agree to at least read the treatment. I hardly let Roy take part in the pitch. I sang songs of casting opportunities, of ideas whose time had come . . .

I finagled Roy into leaving first and I stayed behind and gave it to Krauss, deadpan: like it or not this was the next project in the four-picture deal with Graubart, minus Anne-Marie. Read the contract, I told him. For three days I held my breath, while Krauss undoubtedly sulked and consulted lawyers.

On the fourth day the phone rang at five minutes before midnight. Roy was having an anxiety attack.

"I did my best," I told him. "If they're not totally cold on the war-story angle, there's some hope. Then if I can get them to spend enough development money until they're beyond the point of no return, we're okay. Krauss'll have to go to completed script."

"Okay. I hope you don't mind my calling you this late."

"I would prefer you not to."

"Ha, ha."

Krauss read the treatment himself. My tough stance had gotten us that; not nothing, but not enough. He couldn't believe Graubart was serious.

"Serious enough," I said. "Suppose it had been Anne-Marie who'd turned in this idea?"

"She was a different cup of tea. But Graubart—"

"Just go to a first draft and see what happens. He can pull it off!"

"Why don't you try the networks—they do German stuff on television—you know, *The Winds of War.*"

"Don't do that to me."

"Then offer him the rewrite on the new Steve Martin picture. Steve'll like him. They're both weirdos."

•

I expected the response I got from Roy. "Tell him I said, 'I would prefer not to.'"

"He's not going to get the nuance."

"That's okay. We get it. And Anne-Marie would."

I didn't tell him that if Anne-Marie were alive to pick up nuances, we wouldn't be in this spot. "Listen," I said. "Stay out of Krauss's way—in fact, don't talk to any studio executive. You talk to me and I'll talk to them—till we get this settled."

One of the special bits of extra privilege I'd written into the deal was an office on the lot for Anne-Marie and Graubart. Roy was still in residence. By the end of the next few weeks he was holed up in it, as if it was a bunker at the end of a war.

Krauss offered one more compromise. Any other original Roy wanted, he would okay, sight unseen, up to screenplay—he'd skip the usual step deals.

"He won't do it," I said.

"This guy has an obsession. What is it—was his family wiped out or something?"

"No. No real connection. You're right. It's an obsession."

"Crazy son of a bitch!"

"How about you? Why so generous, all of a sudden?"

"Call it a farewell gift. You're leaving the agency, aren't you?"

"I'm not exactly sure about when."

"Then call it a memorial gift for Anne-Marie. She made a lot of money for us."

"Don't break my heart. What do we do when Graubart says no?"

"The usual. The lawyers'll fight and we'll win. You damn well knew Anne-Marie had cancer when you renegotiated the deal, didn't you?"

"Who knew what would happen? Doctors can do amazing things these days."

Krauss shook my hand with warmth. "So can lawyers," he said.

Roy was unusually silent when I reported all this. I was late for a meeting and left him shaking his head slowly from right to left; not hard to decipher, just hard to answer. He looked a little feverish, flushed.

"Are you okay?' I asked.

Silence and more shaking of the head.

The first hint of the extent of hostilities came when I had my morning coffee and the trades arrived at my desk. On page six of *Daily Variety* there was a description of Graubart's project along with an interview in which Roy brought his friend Bartleby to the attention of Hollywood.

"What the hell are you doing?"

"The best defense—you know."

"How'd you do this? Can you afford a PR firm?"

"A friend owed me a favor. I called it in. And I'm not finished yet."

My other light was signaling—it had to be Krauss—and I got off. He didn't want to talk on the phone; he wanted a meeting in an hour. Not a great sign. There were five people in Krauss's office—count them, five! The story head, two lawyers, and a secretary to take minutes. The more people in a room, the shorter the meeting. Today's meeting would be very brief. Clearly, we were coming to the end of this little comedy. I wasn't surprised at the lawyers. What I'd done with Anne-Marie and Roy had been a coup, a calling in of markers, not a real contract. I always knew it would never stand up if push came to shove. Push was coming to shove.

The lawyers began. "What does your client think he's doing?"

"We don't run our business in the trades."

"This deal does not hold up. You can't inherit a contract."

Krauss held up his hand like a traffic cop.

Quickly, I asked, "Is all this about a little piece in *Daily Variety?* What's the big fuss?"

The fuss, Krauss informed me, was another piece scheduled for tomorrow's *Hollywood Reporter.* And this one was also all about some weird character named Bartleby. There was a rumor that the *L.A. Times* was going to interview Graubart.

"What can I do? Roy's been around. After a while you get to know the press."

"Listen, listen good," Krauss said. "I called your partners and told them what I was going to tell you—so don't be surprised when you get back to your office. We are talking to the Japanese, we are talking to the British, we are talking to the Germans—there's nobody in the world who doesn't have some interest in buying this studio. What we *don't* need is some flaky development deal getting oddball press all over the place. Are you listening? Out— please—your guy is out now!"

His secretary said Roy was at the doctor. I had a call to make at the studio, towards the end of the day, and I stopped by. This was not a conversation I wanted to have on the phone. I had constructed a "worst case" scenario in my mind, and had been torturing myself with it all day. It had Roy-as-Bartleby going to the absolute end: holing up in the office, refusing to move; finding some deep well inside himself which would give him the power, if only for a little while, to tell some of the most powerful people in his world that whatever it was they wished him to do—he preferred not to.

He was lying on the office couch, his eyes closed. He didn't get up or open his eyes while I spoke. When I finished he was quiet for a long while. Then he opened his eyes. I'd never noticed that they were clear blue. One doesn't look closely at someone's eyes unless one of you is in love or in trouble.

"I've been thinking about a couple of years ago when Jellicoe at Metro asked me to rewrite Larry Moon's script, on the sly. Larry was a friend of mine from the old days in New York. We did a soap together: *Days of Our Lives*." He stood up and prowled the office. "'Once, I got a bad case of shingles—they said nobody in their twenties ever got it, but I did. Do you know how killing the pace is on a soap? They're on the air every weekday of the year.

You're out sick for a month or so—and you can lose the whole gig. Anyway, Larry covered for me."

"Energetic friend."

"We were young—but the extra load threw him into overdrive. He ended up screaming at me over coffee at the Carnegie Deli. And we didn't talk for a long time. But the point is—he covered for me. And when the chips were down, all those years later, I rewrote Larry's script for Jellicoe, on the sly, behind Larry's back. Because I didn't want to lose my job."

I sat down in Roy's chair. "Why do I think I know what's coming," I said.

"Because that was the moment—one of a hundred moments—when I should have said—"

"Yes," I said. "I understand." And I told him my fearful scenario of the afternoon—him digging in, scandal, lawyers, maybe even police.

He nodded and lay down on the couch again. "You know me better than I know myself. That's the plan. Something like that."

"Do you have a fever?"

"No," Graubart said. "Just a plan."

"You could take the offer. No steps—any story in the world you want, as long as it's not this one—guaranteed screenplay price. They're being pretty forthcoming."

"You know what the wonderful thing about Bartleby was? He didn't see *their* side of it. Nobody else had a case—no matter how fair or logical they were—they didn't have a case—compared to the fact that he preferred not to. Whatever it was they wanted; no matter how reason-able it might be."

He shook his head. Then he closed his eyes.

I didn't go back to the office, and at home there was a surprise waiting for me. Anne-Marie's lawyers had sent the batch of books she'd left me in her will. It was mostly the kind of stuff our parents would have saved: Robert Musil, Hermann Broch, a few in the original German. I was grateful for the distraction from the explosions threatening the next day. I browsed till I grew drowsy. And when I woke in the morning I knew exactly what I had to do to make everything straight again.

I rehearsed my pitch, as always, on the drive to the studio, this time across Coldwater Canyon. The only way was to fight Bartleby with Bartleby. I was inspired. "Do you realize," I would tell him, "have you analyzed the fact that every request made to Bartleby, to which he makes his famous reply—every one is about business? Nothing is personal! What would he have said if some-one had said, Bartleby, I'm fainting, I'm sick. Please get me a glass of water? Would he still have said: *I would prefer not to?*"

And, having made this point, I would tell him about my partners, about the crisis of my retirement—I would make it clear that any public trouble would strengthen them and weaken me. I would be like a weak father asking for help from a strong son.

Roy was packing papers and scripts. There was debris everywhere.

"Isn't it amazing how much stuff you accumulate in only a few years?" he said.

"Are you feeling better?" It was a foolish question; filler. His feverish flush was gone, the blue eyes clear. He was the old Roy.

"I couldn't do it. I'm getting out. No lawyers, no police, no embarrassing newspaper stuff. They can all relax." His smile was full of regret, the chin pushed up, the mouth curved downwards. "I was always right about myself. I would have told them where my grandmother was hiding if they just squeezed me hard in the right place."

I said, "I'm sorry, Roy."

Later I found out what had happened: the visit from a couple of studio security police, the ultimatum to be out by noon. The security officers did not know they were speaking to a mythical character named Bartleby—they just read Graubart's name on the door and gave him his orders. They were not the SS, just an ex–private detective and a would-be actor, wearing uniforms and performing a routine function. They wore guns in holsters but it's not likely that either of them had ever been used in the line of duty. Roy began to pack as soon as they'd left.

•

Before I left, Graubart surprised me again by grabbing me and pressing a wet cheek against my face. "God, I miss her," he said.

I held him for a long time while he wept for himself in the guise of Anne-Marie. The pitch I'd prepared so carefully, now unnecessary, was limp in my mind. I didn't seem to know any other words. "Yes," I said. And I was filled with disappointment. Even though I was afraid of it, in some way I had also wanted Graubart to play his Bartleby. It would have made awful problems for both of us, a foolish pastiche of an obscure literary character, played out in front of a totally uncomprehending audience. But I wanted somebody to go to the edge, to ransom me, all of us, with this absolute refusal that made no sense except in how absolute it was. My own little charade of father-and-son was finished, too.

Roy was on his own again, as was I.

My two partners and I sat in the same chairs as always at our agency meetings. But this time it was different. They were waiting for my answer—and so was I. Then, quite naturally, as if I'd not spoken my last words in this language when I was fifteen, I said: *"Ich würde lieber nicht."* I had revised the phrase, retranslated it from Anne-Marie's formal elegance. It seemed to me to require a certain brusqueness, a particular simplicity of will. Alvin was the younger one, maybe thirty-seven; Roland was about fifty; both were mystified.

"What's that?" Alvin frowned as if he had a bad connection on a car phone. I repeated the phrase. After that he was startled beyond words. But Roland had some sense of what was going on.

"Well, Herr partner," he said. He flicked his cuffs; the last man in Los Angeles to wear French cuffs and black pearl cufflinks during the business day; a dated sense of style that did not promise well for the future of the agency with or without me.

"Does that mean yes or no?" he asked.

It was a natural question. Even if they both understood German the question would still remain. Depending on others, as we all do, the language of "yes" is our native tongue. The language of refusal, the music of courage, the poetry of "no"—they're all foreign languages; hard to learn.

I leaned forward and, hoping that I was at the beginning of something and not the end, I said, "It means *I would prefer not to.*"

The Man with
the Blue Guitar
by
Wallace Stevens

(a Story by Daniel Stern)

T*HEIR* sudden sexual success surprised them both.
Burnt children of midlife and midtown, they'd tried not to expect too much—sort of a charm against failure. If you don't want what you want too much, maybe they'll give it to you—that sort of thing. When they got it, a fine, tender, savage loveplay triggered by poetry, they were amused, astonished, and grateful, not necessarily in that order.

They'd each been around the track a few times, but no marriages and no kids. Sam was an insurance expediter specializing in disasters: the human and financial aftermath of hurricanes, earthquakes, fires—he'd even covered a tidal wave, once. He lived with one woman for six years, a trial lawyer, and counted that as a disaster. Djinna had a nine years' success with an abstract painter to her credit, even though the man was essentially a son of a bitch.

"Why a success?" Sam asked her.

"Because it had all the ups and downs—all the sideways troubles and getting over things they say you get in a marriage. The sex turned bad for a while, then it got all right again."

"Just all right?"

"It never got back to what it was. He was an angry man. But we weren't kids and we got along. You stop expecting shooting stars after a while. It was a success as those things go."

"But you hung in for almost a decade. And then it didn't last."

"Okay, finally I felt like I'd been in a bad accident, because it ended. Don't complain," she said. "That's why *you're* here."

"Am I here?" he asked. He kissed her, kiddingly, a swipe.

"Sort of. . . . I've been cautious for a while now—afraid of another disaster."

"Disaster's my middle name."

She was too tense to smile. "What worries me," she said, "is I'm just all out of caution," she said. "I've used it up."

She must have meant that she hadn't had an affair in two years or so.

"I'm tapped out," she said.

Sam liked the way she mixed poker lingo with her uptown art gallery style. He kidded her about her talk of being played out, but he was no further along towards taking chances than she was. They were both still in their cautious phase, teasing each other with long sensual bouts, touching everywhere, still clothed, acting the adolescent even though they were both thirty-eight.

"Go home," she would whisper after hours of exhausting play. "I'll be late for my job."

"You hate your job."

It was not true, just deliberate provocation. She managed an art gallery with a specialty in Indian objects— she felt ghettoized but she had a degree in Indian art as well as the regulation red dot on her sweeping brown forehead. She liked the job but often hated dealing with her customers. She took particular pleasure in showing ignorant, patronizing American collectors that she knew which end was up about early Matisse as much as late Kashmir pottery.

Years later, it would be impossible for them to explain how poetry had made their bed a place of happy triumph; or how they'd learned how lucky they were, and how they'd learned that the important thing about luck is not where it comes from but how to make it last.

They'd circled each other for months in the mating dance with the appropriate New York excuses: fatigue, sudden weird job pressures brought on by demanding bosses, crazy clients or colleagues. Finally they had arrived at desperation. For him: bulging flesh, painful scrotum veins, and inability to take anything but short breaths; for her: damp, hypersensitive mucous membranes, painfully stretched open legs, an open bruised and crushed mouth. His eyeglasses were on the living-room floor next to the couch. Hers were shoved up on her forehead. "We're a perfect pair," went a line from his courtship. "You're nearsighted and I'm farsighted. Together we can see the world as it is."

Vision was on Sam's mind right then. He had this odd minor eye problem; odd to the layman, minor to the professional. I'd seen a lot it. Thosis of the eyelids. Nothing more than progressively drooping lids. Bedroom eyes, my mother used to call them. But mine stopped. Sam's kept covering more and more of his field of vision. They were dangerously low. He was having accidents; knocked out some porcelain jacket crowns when he missed seeing a low-hanging bookshelf and smashed his head into it.

We were doing field vision tests and talking about the idea of the operation: no big deal; more like shortening a pair of trouser cuffs than a medical procedure. All this entailed a fair number of office visits and hearing about his Indian maiden and about the long-drawn-out fifties kind of courtship; tender, anxious—kind of comic, it seemed to me as I listened. He hadn't told her about his visual difficulties, yet. But I became an offstage witness to his iambic romance. Now, by my telling this to you, you're in it as well.

Back on the living-room couch Sam rises on one exhausted elbow. He is draped in a confusion of silks: red, maroon, black, pink—scarves from Kashmir, from Bengal country, souvenirs of trips home, each promising an exotic, a fantastic story which Djinna refuses to deliver. That is reserved for the gallery. At home she will not dwell on the old country; an American, now. Yet even the walls are draped with Indian scarves, and carved Kaliesque dancers cast scary shadows late at night. In front of Sam a disheveled Djinna Narayan (pronounced Nar-*ay*-an) paces like Groucho Marx.

"Let me catch my breath." She stood panting in front of some Indian musical instrument hanging on the wall.

"You are the only woman in the world," he says, "who is afraid to make love to a man because it might lead to marriage."

"Shhhh."

"Is this some strange Hindu thing about sex I never heard of?"

"A drink," Djinna said wildly. "That's what I need. Just to ease me off a little."

She rummaged among bottles and searched for ice. It was 1:00 A.M., July in New York. The air conditioner was breathing as hard as Sam and Djinna. All three of them had been at this since ten o'clock. She sat down next to him and transferred a bourbon kiss.

"Oh, God," she said. "It's not working."

Something about the woody taste of bourbon on her tongue made Sam ask her for a poetry anthology.

"What did you say?"

"Poetry. You know, Moon-June . . ."

"Don't be superior. Moon-June is Tin Pan Alley. Which do you want, *The Golden Treasury* or *The Oxford Book of English Verse?*"

"Oxford. I didn't know you read poetry."

"I didn't say I read poetry. I just said I had two anthologies."

"Okay, It's just that nobody reads poetry except college professors, poets, and me."

It's hard to say if the edge of argument cooled her off or kept the temperature up.

He started off with the wrong stuff.

"What lips my lips have kissed , and where, and why
I have forgotten, and what arms have lain
Under my head till morning . . ."

"Oh no," she groaned. Lover's glop. It was Edna St. Vincent Millay. Frankly I think it's quite beautiful. But to Sam and Djinna it was like fumbling foreplay. The anthology was Djinna's body, Sam's fingers touching here, touching there, touching turn-off spots before the turn-on.

He flipped the pages. On the third try he struck it rich: a wild shot.

> *"Call the roller of big cigars,*
> *The muscular one, and bid him whip*
> *In kitchen cups concupiscent curds . . ."*

It might have been the beat that hit below the belt, or it might have been the delicious mixed flavors of the words.

". . . concupiscent curds . . ." she murmured and eased down loosely next to him.

> *"Let be be finale of seem,"* he continued to read.
> *"The only emperor is the emperor of ice cream."*

He jumped at her touch, nervous, unprepared.
After their kiss cracked he said, "Djinna . . ."
She was busy but she murmured, "Yes . . ."
"Is it because English is not your language?"
"Shhhh. Patronizing bastard. *More* . . ."

> *"I should have thought*
> *in a dream you would have brought*
> *some lovely perilous thing,*
> *orchids piled in a great sheath,*
> *as who would say (in a dream)*
> *I send you this,*

who left the blue veins
of your throat unkissed. "

He thought she was going berserk, trembling with animal sounds. Could that language she was moaning far inside her throat be Hindi? He made the mistake of asking her. She clubbed him on the side of the head and then kissed the bruise.

"Idiot! Do you think everything unexpected that happens to me is because I'm a foreigner?"

"I didn't know. You're my first Indian."

"I wasn't talking. I was responding. Like a cat or a dog."

"Don't be paranoid."

"I'm not. Americans all hate Indians. Much worse than the British. You think I don't see that?"

The air conditioner started choking. He made an instinctive jerk towards it. She buried herself in corners of his body he didn't know he had—he was bony, tall—he had angles, not deep corners.

"No," she said. "I don't care about air conditioning. Read some more."

In a haste of panic he started in the middle of a page:

"*His true Penelope was Flaubert,*
He fished by obstinate isles;
Observed the elegance of Circe's hair
Rather than the mottoes on sun-dials. "

She dropped from the couch, in a crunch of sound, to crouch next to him keeping one hand where it was; the other steadied her fall. She was careless of everything except not jostling the book sitting on his chest. She draped him in a sheet of blackest hair. For the moment he was a passive lover. However excited he might get, now was the moment of the imperial command: READ!

He read.

> *"I am afraid to own a body,*
> *I am afraid to own a soul;*
> *Profound, precarious property,*
> *Possession not optional."*

It was time to drop the book, time to pick up Djinna. She shifted as Sam reached for her and he heard a crunch, a shock of glass.

"Did you break—?"

"I don't know—I guess . . ."

"Did you cut—?"

"I don't know—I don't care."

He picks her up and swings her towards him, smearing red streaks on the white couch, and bends to kiss, first, the bloody knees, then the brown field of stomach, the fork of legs, and at last he lets the book drop among the scattered shards of glass.

Djinna laughed and sucked up the broken glass with a small hand vacuum.

"My God," she said. "What bloody carnage."

"The wars of poetry," Sam said. "I knew a poet at

Columbia. I used to wonder why he was so tough. Now I know. You can get hurt playing with poetry."

He made her lie still, knees clamped, while he dabbed alcohol and felt for tiny needles of trouble.

"That was astonishing," Djinna said. "I was nowhere and everywhere at the same time."

"It was terrific. Hold still."

"Who was that second one you read?"

"I wasn't counting—H. D., I think. I'll get you her collected poems."

"No." She closed her eyes against the alcohol sting. "I don't want to read it. I just want you to read it to me." She opened her satisfied eyes. He extracted the final sliver.

"Owwww."

"I thought you liked her."

"My mother always said men are cruel afterwards. The alcohol stings."

"Her real name is Hilda Doolittle."

"How come she could do what Jack Daniel's couldn't?"

He thought a moment, soberly, as if the question meant something important to him, too.

"It's all a question of feet. H. D. has better feet than the best bourbon in the world."

Djinna drew her long skirt down over her knees.

"What do you mean—feet?"

"That's what they call the beats of rhythm in poems. You know—'The *boy* stood *on* the *burn*ing *deck*.' Can't you hear the footsteps? A pulse?"

"No." She stood up abruptly, ready to get on with real life. "Let's clean up and go out for dinner," she said. "Where are my glasses?"

He reached up and pulled them down from the nest of her hair where they usually lived.

A few nights later Sam arrived at her apartment a half hour late because he'd been at my office for one last field vision test. He'd come to me, originally, because we'd been quite friendly at Dartmouth and I'm an ophthalmic plastic surgeon; this eyelid number is one of our small specialties. That night the test was actually performed with the eyelids Scotch-taped up, to see how the world looked with his usually drooping eyelids providing a decent opening for once. He told me it had been like a startling starry night to be able to see those little sun and star bursts against the black field—to see them with such clarity. A joy! Except that it probably meant he should have the operation. That was enough of a drag so that Sam didn't mention it to Djinna. He didn't want to spoil things.

There was a lot to spoil. Djinna was waiting for him like a bride in a fairy tale, only instead of holding flowers or a love potion she held *The Oxford Book of English Verse.*

> *"That's my last duchess painted on the wall,*
> *Looking as if she were alive. I call*
> *That piece a wonder, now . . ."*

Djinna brushed her lips across his forehead.

"I read that when I was a kid," Djinna said. "It's about marriage."

"More about jealousy, power," Sam said. "Everybody

reads poetry when they're kids. But we're the only grown-ups, minus students and poets, in the whole world who are reading it now. I should shut up and not tempt fate with so much self-satisfied pride, right?"

She stretched out on his lap, face up. Her gown parted, shadowed, above the knees, dark, like a bend in a river. "Let's tempt the gods," she said. "Let's be smug and self-satisfied. Let's give a new meaning to the words 'reading for pleasure.' "

"Okay—no dinner, tonight. Anything will do."

"Nothing will do."

"That's what I meant."

He opened the book at random.

Her gown parted a little more as if by its own will. He reached one hand down towards the shadows.

She guided his hand. "Come down here."

"Come up here."

"Come here."

"You come *here.*"

They struggled and each gave in, though not at the same time.

Immediately afterward she ignored all the echoes and rhythms at which she'd trembled a few moments before. "I'm starved," she said.

"Okay," he said. "No afterplay. What's there to eat?"

Apparently there was everything in the world: a spread of temptations spanning oceans as well as cookbooks. Curried chicken, glazed ham, chopped liver, undefined salads—they devoured them ferociously, tearing chicken legs from bones, ripping instead of slicing rye bread; she giggled at their hungers and made a joke about the *Tom Jones* movie, some famous scene in which the man and woman feast on food instead of each other, staring at each other all the while—so as to clue the audience into the food-for-sex substitution.

Sam opened the refrigerator and searched for an open bottle of wine, a Coke, anything.

"That," he said, "is such baloney. It's a metaphor for a damned puritanical culture."

"Don't lecture me," Djinna said, laughing. "Get me something to drink, too."

"Devouring chicken instead of each other. What a lie. It's a perversion worse than anything in Krafft-Ebing."

"Who?"

"Never mind. The point is, you feast on food *after* sex. Not instead of. That's the way it's supposed to be."

"You don't have to convince me. Just get me a beer."

Sam bent down quickly, reaching for a cold bottle, and the minute the refrigerator door left his field of vision he slammed his head into it with ferocious force. I had warned him, after the first series of accidents, never to bend down quickly. He told this to Djinna, a few minutes later, when she was cradling his head and pressing ice cubes onto a brutal bump.

"Why shouldn't you bend down for a beer?" she asked, and he gave her the nickel tour of the whole "bedroom eyes," field-of-vision routine; the lighthearted version. But when he got to the accidents, one of which she'd just witnessed, she was angry. "How could you not tell me?"

"Everything has been too good. I didn't want to spoil things."

"You think if you close your eyes it'll go away."

"Bad jokes. Besides, there's a small operation for it. My guy says it's about as complex as taking up a pants cuff."

"Ha. Is this tailor any good?"

"He's better, he's careful. I've known him for years. I had an examination this afternoon, before I came here. He's unusually smart; collects rare art."

"A cultivated doctor. The worst kind. What's the next step? That was awful not seeing the refrigerator shelf."

"I'm going to have the operation."

But pleasure and eyelid shortening would both have to wait while Sam headed out for California in the wake of a small earthquake. Just a five point three but there was damage; there were claims to be adjusted, troubled people to listen to, reports to be written.

Alone at the Holiday Inn in Hermosa Beach he noted that he had not brought any poetry to read. For years Sam had traveled with a small paperback anthology of English and American poems. Usually an old, out-of-print Oscar Williams, beat up but companionable. Dumb, he thought, turning his long avocation over so completely to Djinna. A grown-up version of adolescents cherishing "their" song. How embarrassing! He grinned wetly as he brushed his teeth in the plastic bathroom. Was reading a poem alone now going to be a new form of masturbation?

Sam was convinced that this phenomenon, this discovery of a new fuel for passion, would never have ignited in the same way with an American woman. "Snob," Djinna said the next evening over the curried shrimp appetizer. "No," he defended himself. "Americans have no poetic culture behind us. No great saga. Just 'Trees' by Joyce Kilmer. We're pure prose." She'd met him at the door with a kiss, a vodka and the promise of a surprise after dinner. Dinner itself was a surprise. They were going out.

"We can't just keep feeding on each other," she said, putting on her glasses so she could read the menu.

"Why not? I've been away for a week. I'm hungry."

"Try the tandoori chicken," she said, swerving sweetly.

"I thought you didn't like the way they do Indian food in America."

"I want you to get to know it," Djinna said. "It's the best food in the world. And doing something good, doing it okay, but not quite wonderfully, is better than not doing it at all."

Like a kid, he asked, "Where's my surprise?"

But that would come after dinner, back at her apartment. In the half-lit bedroom, great multicolored pillows on the floor to avoid the threatening formality of a bed, she showed him the poem she wanted, with the verses she wanted him to read.

"Choosing your own aphrodisiac?" Sam scowled.

"Never examine good luck too closely. Just read."

"Is that an Indian proverb?"

"All except the last two words. Just read."

"We'll get our names into the psychology textbooks. We've discovered the first middle-class perversion."

"READ!"

He began, "The man . . ."

"No." She pointed. "Start there. I want to jump around."

> *"They said, You have a blue guitar,*
> *You do not play things as they are."*
>
> *The man replied, "Things as they are*
> *Are changed upon the blue guitar."*
>
> *And they said then, "But play, you must,*
> *A tune beyond us, yet ourselves."*

She crouched next to him, not languorous, coiled this time, for some reason. This one was *her* discovery. "Beyond us, yet ourselves," she murmured. He kissed her and she surprised him then, reaching for the book. She had always wanted him to read the rhythms, the images. Now she spoke them:

> *Throw away the lights, the definitions,*
> *And say of what you see in the dark."*

He stopped listening and played at being Djinna, registering half-phrases while he undressed her, indeed, looking at the shadows of her brown nipples, kissing the well of her parting legs. He kept certain phrases—"the madness of space" . . ."jocular procreations". . . She moved this way and that to make his task easier while reading. But finally, for reasons of her own, she handed the book back to him, in time for the last two lines. She had better uses for her hands than holding books.

You as you are? You are yourself.
The blue guitar surprises you.

That was the night Sam finally told her about his ex—the trial lawyer, Nadine; six years of waiting for the jury to come in, affection always conditional—on how the day's cases went, on how fiery his attentions were.

"I'm not so different from her," Djinna said.

"Just day and night. She had no staying power."

"I thought it's the man who has to—"

"Get your mind out of the gutter, Narayan."

She laughed, happily. "Just afterplay."

"Wrong," he said, bending down with great caution to find a plate of cold chicken. "This is our afterplay."

Solemnly she said, "Some people smoke. We head for the refrigerator."

"Nadine was a holy terror. Each time we made love it was a test."

"That's a tough school to graduate from."

"I don't know why I ever thought we'd get married. With you it just seems the natural next step."

Djinna stood up, beer can in hand.

"How natural?" she asked.

He told her that nothing concentrates one's thoughts of the future like contemplating the imminent or distant doom of the entire state of California, while lying on a bed in a motel room in Hermosa Beach. At such moments futures are decided.

And so it was decided. But the threat of the operation troubled her. When would he have it done? Before the wedding? If not, how long after? Sam, she pointed out, was not a pair of trousers and his eyelids were not cuffs.

"Let's not hang the man for a metaphor."

"I'd like to meet this doctor," Djinna said. But when Sam told her my name she stammered a bit and seemed upset and the notion of a meeting was quickly dropped. Two days later Sam was filling out pre-op forms at my office and he brought up the incident. I told him the truth at once—that we'd gone out once or twice.

"Was it once or twice?"

"Twice, I think. A couple of years ago. I was in my expanding collecting phase and India was on my mind. We met at the gallery, then we had a drink, and one thing led to nothing."

"If it was such a nothing why didn't you mention it all these weeks I've been telling you about her?"

"*Because* it was nothing. Also, frankly, you jumped into these intimate conversations so quickly, I was a little embarrassed. I'm a WASP—my family never confides or talks about intimacies so lightly. It just seemed—I don't know—gauche to intrude myself into this story. I'm sorry if—"

"No, no," Sam said. "I'm Jewish, she was born a Hindu, and you're a WASP. There's no sorting this out. I'll take your word for it."

"Okay, I think you're dilated now. Lean forward."

You must understand, there was something perfectly

pure in the way he told me about this poetry-as-passion-maker. He told it from the first in the most wondering way, with all the respect due a miraculous conversion. I was examining his optic nerve, after our tense discussion of my having gone out with Djinna, when he said, "There's something magic about all this. Last night it was Wallace Stevens."

"Really. Which?"

" 'The Man with the Blue Guitar.' Do you realize there have been a hundred million words published to prove that Stevens is a dry, unsensuous, intellectual poet?"

"You mean," I said, blunt as is my way, "that his balls are all in his head."

But like all new lovers, he was unshakable.

"Apparently not," he said. A satisfied smile appeared in the beam cast by my examination light.

I shut it off. "The optic nerve is healthy," I told him. "All the signs are good. My secretary will set you up next week. It will take less than an hour."

Sam raised the question of getting married before or afterwards.

"It doesn't matter. You may feel a little scratchiness, like having a speck in your eye, that first evening. And that's it."

"You're sure. Because I can take some discomfort now—but after the wedding I just want—bliss."

They decided to get married, quickly. City Hall was closer than New Delhi and Sacramento, where their families lurked in the jungles and freeways of the past. They could go west and east later, for more leisurely formalities. The trick was to get it started. They would honeymoon, after the operation, in India or California. It didn't much matter which, as long as one poetry collection or another went along.

I'm sure you've guessed that something went wrong with the procedure—the "operation." No, nobody's blind or permanently injured. It was bad enough without melodrama. Doctors have a saying, when something goes awry, you can bet it's a relative or a friend. During the procedure, Sam worried us, once. He moved his head powerfully enough, during the stitching, to make the vise that held his head tremble a bit. But the rest of the operation was uneventful. Djinna sat outside, waiting to take Sam home. She'd said, "Hello, how have you been," when they'd arrived, polite but cool, acknowledging that we knew each other and, as well, couragously risking the use of my first name.

Afterwards, she was all attention to Sam. He sat like a soldier for the prescribed half hour; he looked like a soldier, too, I suppose, with both of his eyes patched. Anyway, there was no shock, no allergic reaction. A smooth show. Until a couple of hours later, at home, when it all started. The anesthetic wore off. Djinna unpatched his eyes, as per my instructions. He tried to open his eyes: *excruciating pain—and he couldn't open them.*

The italics are mine, because I want you to get this from Sam's viewpoint; which was an astonishment of anguish. And like most people, he'd always been able to open his eyes when he wished to. That was an astonishment of helplessness. The combination was unbeatable.

As soon as Djinna called me and told me what had happened, I knew what he was experiencing. When they got to the office, which I opened at nine o'clock at night, stifling because the air conditioning had been off since six, I examined him. There were corneal abrasions over ninety percent of both eyes.

I was as astonished as Sam and Djinna. I had never heard of anything like this. Correction, I dimly recalled one case where something had gone wrong—but that was years ago, in the procedure's infancy. I put a few drops of anesthetic in each eye and I could see Sam's eyes open, wet, gooey from the drops and from the antibiotic salve I'd squirted in earlier.

"Oh," Sam murmured. "Thank God. That feels wonderful. What went wrong?"

I didn't know. He might have been allergic to the sutures or to the chemicals the sutures were soaked in. But it didn't really matter. The abrasions would heal themselves. When they came back the next day I gave them both the standard cornea lecture—how it's made in layers and the eye gradually heals the corneal surface, layer by layer, until finally there would little or no discomfort. But it could be weeks or months.

"The only prescription," I told Djinna, as they left again, "is tincture of time."

In the meantime Sam was in hell. Every few hours the anesthetic would wear off and his eyes would shut down as if onto hot coals. By the fourth day I did something no doctor should ever do. I gave Sam a bottle of the anesthetic, with strict instructions not to overuse. If he *had* overused the stuff, he could have ruined his vision forever. But by that time, we were all feeling a little desperate. Djinna tended him day and night.

"What happened to your famous Indian edginess?" Sam whispered to her, lying down with a damp cloth covering his eyes. "You're a saint."

"I'm not; I'm just married to you now. I'm a Jewish wife in the presence of pain. And Indians are not typically edgy, you racist bastard. It's just *me.*" She kissed him carefully around the mouth. "But, if you remember, it only takes a little poetry to take a lot of the edges off."

In the meantime, she read poems to him; new stuff she had discovered. Neither of them could tell, in these grotesque new circumstances, whether the erotic thrust was still there. It was a holding action—memory of pleasures against present pain. The real stuff would have to wait.

She read:

> *"For everything that's lovely is*
> *But a brief, dreamy kind delight."*

Later he woke from a fortunate doze and commented that they should have gone to visit her family for a honeymoon. "Instead of this."

"There are people who look the way you do, now, lying all over the streets in New Delhi."

They made some wit out of his anguish and by Labor Day a sublime coolness struck the city like a benediction.

Simultaneously Sam's pain subsided. The city could begin to breathe again and the cornea was repairing itself. It was about this time, apparently, that Sam felt well enough to make love again. But his eyes were not up to the sustained effort of reading to Djinna; they were dry and he found it difficult to focus. Everything went wrong. Nothing mechanical, and nothing technical. It was just not the same magic.

The first day in which Sam needed no medication and no anesthetic he tried another tack—reciting a poem from memory, while touching Djinna.

"The book of moonlight is not written yet."

She moved with solemn tenderness under his words and his hands and they were satisfied and happy—but quite different. Before, the passion had seemed an end in itself, and it grew wilder with the words he read. The ultimate satisfaction was actually a surprise when it finally arrived. It was as if, like children, they'd had no idea of the consequences of what they were doing. Each time they were taken by surprise—holding each other, damp and exhausted, with smiles that said, "Well, look what happened to us," almost sorry that it was over.

Now, as he recited, passing the poems only past his memory not his eyes, some peculiar part of the recipe was missing. Everything was delicious, but they tasted different to each other. So they murmured, afterwards, of shock and trauma and tincture of time and honey-

moons to come and walked in the fall coolness to sear
their mouths with curry and cool them with yogurt at a
favorite Indian restaurant.

"You know," Sam said, "it wasn't just you as a woman
responding to poetry—the male eye and voice as key and
the female as the lock to be opened. Something in me
opened, too."

"I know," she said, hopeless. "Maybe the gods are
punishing me. Didn't I say that if something is good, then
doing it just okay but not quite wonderfully is all right?"

"Did you say that ?"

"I meant making Indian food—but the gods get things
wrong, sometimes."

"Don't they," Sam said.

Djinna was the first to seek me out, afterwards. I'd been
seeing both of them, together, of course, for the regular
convalescent office visits. She'd told Sam some story about
an appointment with a private dealer in the East Eighties,
which is where my office is.

"You didn't want him to know you were coming here?"

"No."

"Why not?"

"I'm not sure. I'm a little shaken up."

"That's natural. Just married and suddenly you're
leading your husband into and out of taxis and emergency rooms."

It took a while before she actually came out and asked
me the prognosis. I reminded her of my famous cornea
lecture, et cetera.

"And that's all?" she pressed me.

I also reminded her that she and Sam could seek out a second opinion. But he seemed to me to be on the healing track.

"None of this explains why you didn't tell Sam about coming here."

It all came out, then. As delicately as she could, she clued me in on a passionate life, premarriage, driven by Sam's reading of poems. It cost her something to tell me about it. Djinna had a sharp, New York art gallery veneer, but there was something of the India-maiden about her beneath that. Not the first shy person to come on super-smart, I suppose. I said nothing about how much I already knew.

Then she told me the new stuff—post-trauma. The disappointments, the change. It turns out her real question was pseudomedical. Could there be some connection between the awful abrasion of Sam's eyes, this painful experience, and the consequent downslide in their intimate life. She tied herself in knots to make sure I didn't get the idea that she was complaining. Their life—new and old—was wonderful and they were both very much in love. But neither of them knew anything about medicine, or science, for that matter.

"That's some question, rolling the universe in a ball and throwing it at someone, for an answer."

"Is that a quotation? A poem?" She frowned.

"If it is it's garbled. Anyway, passion is so absolutely personal . . . like fingerprints . . . no two alike anywhere in the world. . . . But there is certainly no clinical connection between the eyes and—other parts."

"I'm not talking about parts. I think you're missing—"

"No, no I'm not. If we're talking about trips to the moon—everyone wants them, has them sometimes, and then not other times."

"But why should it be because he couldn't read—"

She draped her sari around long legs and stared at the floor as if confessing to something perverted.

"It sounds crazy," Djinna said.

"Well, you could always go to an analyst—or one of those family-therapy people."

She smiled her first smile that I'd seen in months. "We've talked about that. But we're still in the middle of a mystery. There's's always time for commonsense therapy, later."

"You know, Djinna," I said, "some people might think the whole thing was crazy."

She looked directly at me. "I think not most people. Most would think we were just—lucky."

"Then maybe this is just unlucky."

I felt like Mephistopheles in some cheap production of Faust. A summer-stock Mephisto cruelly pressing the unfortunate laws of the universe on some poor amateur Faust—well, in this case, some poor Marguerite. I stood up. Doctors often stand up, have you noticed, when they're going to make an authoritative pronouncement.

"If it's just luck—then luck can change," I told her. "It goes both ways, good and bad, an endless pendulum."

I walked her to the door. "In any case Sam will soon be able to see and read as well as ever."

When the door closed behind her, I felt angry, as if I'd been badly used. I didn't exactly understand why.

•

When Sam called and asked to see me, alone, it was almost comic; the two of them circling each other with me in the middle. I decided to see him at the end of the office day, to somehow try to draw a line between the professional and the personal. This case, if that was what it was, was becoming complicated. It turned out that he was on his way out of town for the first disaster since his own.

"An oil refinery in Oklahoma City," Sam said, settling onto my couch. "It exploded a week ago—and everything's still burning. Its's good to get back to making a living."

"It sounds satisfyingly awful. I'm sure they'll need you."

"I'm sure. The way my associate at the office described it, it may be the worst of my ill-starred career." Sam laughed. "This one," he said, "will teach me the meaning of the word 'suffering.' "

I made the obligatory remarks about not selling his own pain short, but I was glad to see him getting some perspective on his surgical aftermath. As it developed, I was glad too soon. Since he was traveling, I took the occasion to tell him, in greater detail than before, how corneal abrasions can recur, once you've had them.

"For no reason?"

"Sometimes the eyelid is not completely closed at night and the cornea dries out—and presto!"

"You mean more abrasions—and pain!"

I didn't care for his sound, and I gave him a pocketful

of lubricating ointment samples to use every night, without fail. I told him to fill up his eyes with protective goop.

"Won't that blur my vision?"

"Do it just before sleep."

"Suppose I want to read or something."

"You mean read *to* somebody?"

"I see you remember," Sam said. He was on the verge of a reconfession, and I was not ready for it.

"Just use it when you're drifting off," I said and then told him that I could use a drink and the Carlyle was practically around the corner, the home of killer martinis in the grand style. . . .

I had to get us out of my office because I felt less and less in control. I would do better at the Carlyle. By the second drink Sam was less tense and all too ready to tell me about the diminished wonder in the bedroom. "Diminished" was the actual word he used and reused. Essentially he told the same story Djinna had. Paradise not exactly Lost but Changed. The Garden of Eden turned into, well, into an ordinary garden; where certain flowers bloom, others wither, perhaps die, and some are perennial. It's called life, I told Sam.

I don't mean to be unsympathetic but I have been married twice, once with great joy. She died in her thirties and left me to the mercies of a world full of bad choices, one of which I proceeded to make, and unmake, almost immediately.

Thus, I'm something of a veteran of the pleasures and losses of the emotional and sexual life. Like a lot of people who didn't wait as long as Sam and Djinna to get married. I was getting a little weary of the implied—or not so implied—accusation that this little procedure of ours which had taken an impossible-to-predict bad turn was responsible for the blighting of our cross-cultural Héloise and Abelard. No, that's a bad one—didn't they castrate him? Let's say Romeo and what's-her-name; worse, too young. Well, you get the idea.

"It has been not been a wonderful time," Sam said.

"It would have diminished anyway, you know."

"How can you be sure?"

"I was married; also I'm a doctor. Married or single—everything diminishes. It's a law of life." I beckoned for the waiter. A pianist, not the famous one, had begun to play show tunes. "I know that's cold comfort."

"Right," Sam said. He was happy to see the waiter and ordered another martini. "Warm comfort's the only kind I'm interested in right now. Besides, I thought change was the only law."

"Same thing."

The fresh round arrived and, as if we were in some sort of competition, we polished them off faster than the first batch.

"Are you saying that change equals less? Is that your idea?"

"It's not my idea. Oh, hell, Sam, these philosophical disquisitions aren't helping anything."

"Besides," Sam pressed forward with the special relentlessness you see in wounded patients, the energy of hurt and injustice powering his wind and voice, "because it would have happened later, *might* have happened later, doesn't make what we've lost in the meantime any less precious. Does it?"

"You're right, Sam," I said. I was glad to be having this conversation anyplace except in my office; here I could hide behind another and another frosty glass, and the sweet, silly sounds of the cocktail piano seemed to bridge the abyss we were both gazing into, from different sides. "Yes," I said, flatly. "I would guess it makes it *more* precious. It was a lame, dumb remark, and I'm sorry."

"Tell me, one thing I meant to ask. Why didn't you try one eye, first, and do the second one later, when all had gone well?"

Helplessly, I said, "I don't know. It's such a simple, safe procedure that I didn't think of that."

Behind the *vino* was lurking some concealed *veritas*, and I let it out, at that moment, surprising both of us. I told him how sorry I was for what had happened. By a great effort of will I left out every easy trick of amelioration with which doctors, surgeons in particular, get through a life. I was a traitor to my profession, for a moment, and put his unexpected and unwarranted suffering at the center of my speech, entirely at the center of the universe.

Sam thanked me and raised his glass in what he undoubtedly took to be a gesture of final absolution. I'm certain, too, that he assumed my apology to be all-inclusive, medical gaffe and intimate loss—the works. The truth is, I confess *I never believed that they'd found this unique bed of poems.* Italics mine.

And it followed that I certainly did not believe that Sam's temporary pain and blindness could make it collapse—or at least sag—beneath the weight of their passion. But we silently toasted our different visions of what had occurred, and Sam, in a large gesture, offered to pay the check, but I persuaded him to order one last round. (I had no surgery scheduled for forty-eight hours. That's my rule: forty-eight hours.)

"I did something lousy," Sam said, finally. "To Djinna."

"It's been a hard time. I'd recommend six months, judgment-free."

"Easy to say."

"What did you do?"

"I hit below the belt. I read her some lines from 'The Blue Guitar'—the piece that was like our anthem—stuff out of context. . . ." Sam closed his eyes, in the artifical, permanent twilight of the bar, and quoted:

> *"Things as they are have been destroyed.*
> *Have I? Am I a man that is dead*
>
> *At a table on which the food is cold?"*

"I mean, is that a low blow, or what, to a woman who is trying to put everything back together again?" Sam signed the credit card slip and started to gather things, scarf, gloves.

"It comes out as a lot of self-pity."

"That's what I had in mind. Unfair to the woman, to the poet, both."

When he told me what she did in response, I waited for his cue and when he laughed I joined in and that was how we parted, laughter and forgiveness having passed between us, each convinced that he understood how the other felt.

At Sam's final checkup I discharged him. He was still a touch anxious about the future and I told him he should have no more ill effects. However, I did tell him that he would probably have a certain residual dryness, for years, possibly always. I advised the frequent use of artificial tears, over the counter in any drugstore, during the day and the ointment at night. He brought up nothing more personal and neither did I and we said goodbye.

Still, for weeks, even months, I found it hard to shake the whole matter off. I actually reread "The Man with the Blue Guitar" and even, God help us, some critics who wrote about it. One line got to me: "The blue guitar surprises Stevens as it surprises us, and we ought to remember that to be 'surprised' means to be captured or to be taken hold of without warning." And, of course, isn't that what everyone wants? Perhaps, after all, they had found and lost some special sensual surprise of good luck enjambed in feet and images which would account for Djinna's action when Sam used a stanza of "The Blue Guitar" to dramatize his self-pity. Sam had told me that she was in such a rage that she threw the book at him. Apparently it's not just an expression.

It hit him in the eyes, but there was no damage. Later, of course, she apologized, she may even have wept. But they were married for a long time after that, more or less happily.

I believe they still are, though by now we've lost touch.

The Communist
Manifesto
by Karl Marx and
Friedrich Engels

(a Story by Daniel Stern)

Until now the philosophers have only tried to
understand the world . . . the point, however, is
to change it. —*Karl Marx*

The point is not to change the world. All the
worst people change the world. The point is to
understand it. —*Maurice Marx*

B*IXBY*, Mettro, Manishin, and Marx.

Ah, Bixby, Mettro, Manishin, and Marx. Sitting here in my high-ceilinged underpriced West End Avenue co-op, waiting for my wife to come by and leave the keys for the last time, I am giving a party in my head. A party for Bixby, Mettro, Manishin, and Marx: for all the soldiers of my formative years, the shock troops of my imagination—the drill sergeants of my character and achievements; the Unknown Soldiers of my finest failures. One glass is all I need for this party. It is full of ice and yellowish vodka, colored and flavored by a spear of buffalo grass. I raise it to my guests, one by one, each of whom had a key point about the living of life to impart; points I seem somehow to have missed.

Bixby, sword-skinny, wild-blond hair, long, long fingers gesticulating, apparently independent of each other and the hands to which they were attached; Bixby wearing the remnants of an Air Force uniform he'd never been issued, and whose age remained a mystery—he could have been anything from twenty-two to forty. Vitamins, he said, vitamins were the secret, he took thirty-eight different pills a day. Thin as a skeleton, but a healthy, energetic skeleton. Depression-prone, Bixby shone with a mad optimism; optimism about playing the piano; those lighter-than-air fingers were self-taught and full of dazzling technique—optimism about writing the Second Great

American Marxist Science Fiction Novel (he had already written the first, but its whereabouts were a mystery buried in the puzzles of piles of old *Cosmos* magazines, in which it had been serialized)—even optimism about Dianetics. Bixby was one of the first "clears" in a still muddy America, long before Dianetics had become the menacing Church of Scientology; optimism extending even to the coming triumph of Marxist Socialism and the possibilities of a revival of interest in the works of Scriabin.

All things were harmonized in Bixby. When you were in his presence there seemed to be no contradiction between the tight constructions of Marxist thought, the wild fantastic leaps of Dianetics, and the heated sevenths and ninths of Scriabin.

Mettro and Manishin, too, turned out to have their own weird take on Marxist Thought. No, not Thought. Everything, then, was how to *live* life—what to *do!* Not merely what to think. Thought as a possible way of being was an old story in Europe. But it wasn't due in America until years later. For the moment the streets were packed with Marxist madmen and madwomen—knowing and unknowing; all set on changing the world one way or another. Everybody was hellbent on the Unity of Theory and Practice! (Otherwise known as "If you think it but can't *do* it something is wrong.") We'd just won a war. It gave us the idea that we could make things work.

I was one year out of the Army, a passionate student of drawing at the Art Students League, of creative writing at the New School for Social Research. The more credits I enrolled for, the more money I got on the G.I.

Bill—plus more textbooks to sell on the open market. How serious was I about drawing and writing? Well, you decide! And bear in mind the fact that I also managed to squeeze in an enrollment at the Arthur Murray Dance Studio in Washington Heights. The first ballroom dance studio to be accredited by the naive, guilt-ridden, postwar U.S. Government.

Bixby was from Indiana. Mettro was from too many places to count, but California was the basic starting point. He was studying public relations at the New School in the evening, the cool spring 1947 evenings. That was something new you could do then, *study* to be in public relations. During the day Mettro fixed cars. He was frail, dark, and Jewish, but being from California he naturally knew all you could know about cars. When he was ten Mettro had taken apart a Pontiac and put it back together, landing on network radio in the process. He also loved music, his specialty being early twentieth century. Which was how I got to meet Bixby. Mettro was watching me dance one evening at the Arthur Murray School. He sat smoking his Gauloises and observing my attempts to get as close as I could to the young southern lady who was teaching me to move, keeping exactly a forearm's length between our bodies. At the piano the still unknown Bixby played waltzes, rumbas, even congas, as richly textured as if he were being paid by the note. On the floor I counted 1-2-3-4 and tried to engage Miss Surrey's eyes with mine. After having failed at this for twenty minutes I took a break and bummed a Gauloise from Mettro.

"Bad luck," I said.

"Did you hear the pianist?"

"I'm talking about Miss Surrey."

"Never mind; listen to that pianist. He's playing Scriabin. I can't believe it. 'The Poem of Ecstasy' in waltz time, 'The Poem of Ecstasy' in rumba time, 'The Poem of Ecstasy' in conga time." He was right. The next time I was on the floor I forgot about my frustration and listened in amazement. It was a virtuoso dazzlement of notes and rhythms all, indeed, based on that luxuriant hothouse piece by the mad Russian.

Miss Surrey, for all her distant southern charm, could not compete. Mettro and I waited till the end of the session. By the time a porter danced across the empty floor with a broom, Bixby, in his mélange of uniform parts from various services topped off with a snappy Air Force officer's cap, was ours. Scriabin brought us together like old friends. Only Miss Surrey could keep us apart. He had a date with the dancing belle. By the time it was clear that he had been stood up it was almost midnight.

"Screwed again," Bixby sighed. "As it were."

"Get your music," Mettro said. "We'll have a drink."

"I don't use music."

"Never?"

"I can't read it."

"*Incroyable,*" Mettro said. He had been in France when the war ended and had a few souvenirs to show. "On that, I'll buy the drinks." And off we went to midtown Manhattan where drinks could be had to celebrate new admirations, new friendships.

Actually, I must pause to tell you that we did not end up at a bar, we bought, much more characteristic of those days, hamburgers and coffee, right there in ugly old Washington Heights. This is not an idle digression. The point is—I almost changed Hamburger Harry's, in which the sawdust was so wet you had to walk very carefully, into a chic midtown bar, martinis, scotch, and all. The truth is—and the whole thing about not missing the point is truth, isn't it?—the truth is this pseudo-Marxist trick of presenting earlier experiences in the style of later ones is absolutely terrible. Whether it's Trotsky the hero of the Revolution becoming Trotsky the counterrevolutionary monster, or a hamburger joint becoming a chic cocktail lounge, it screws up the possibility of ever learning anything. Which is one of the reasons I am sitting here, surrounded by suitcases, entertaining ghosts.

"All those notes," I marveled to Bixby.

Bixby popped vitamin pills and drank vegetable juice.

"The more notes I play, the more they pay me. They want quantity, I give quantity. For myself, I get it back by using Scriabin."

Scriabin, he told us, was a great unsung genius of modern times and his day would come. As for Miss Surrey, he was not too concerned about her disappearance. It seemed that Bixby was impotent, a dark result of some shadowy experience in the war in which he had never taken part, whose uniform he had bought in army surplus stores. Instant converts to Bixby-Scriabin, we did not question. This did not mean that we believed him With his wild blue eyes, his dramatically high cheekbones—a legacy from a Welsh grandfather and an American Indian grandmother—he compelled suspension of disbelief. We suspended, willingly.

Two days later, after my Creative Writing class, there was Bixby waiting for me.

"I heard the story you read," he said. "You're going to be good."

"I don't know," I said.

"I know. Listen, lend me eighteen bucks, will you? I've got to see somebody," he said mysteriously. The oddness of the number disarmed me. I complied.

"Thanks," he said, "I'll give it back to you tomorrow at my office." Office? There was, then, a daytime Bixby?

The office turned out to be *Cosmos Science Fiction Magazine*. Now as solid as the Smithsonian Institution, *Cosmos* was then struggling to be heard, as was science fiction itself. Bixby was passionate about this, as about so many things. Surrounded by empty typewriter chairs and desks—it was the end of the work day—he expatiated on his Science Fiction Marxist vision. Karl Marx and Friedrich Engels had sounded the first note in *The Communist Manifesto*. The note of the unreality of modern experience. If I was going to be a writer—and I was, Bixby had decided—I had better listen to that note.

"Unreality," I said. "Marx and Engels?" It was as close as I could come to a challenge. I was on uncertain ground. Because of a certain secret involving my family, I had never read much by the big Marxist thinkers, including

Numero Uno, the big KM himself. It was an inhibition I think you'll understand later on; around page sixty, I think.

But now, the word "unreality" seemed to light a fire under Bixby. He leaped up and ran up and down the room past a row of jumbled books. Finally he extricated a ragged soft-covered book—as much pamphlet as book—and opened it.

"Listen to this," he said. He read:

"Constant revolutionizing of production, uninterrupted disturbance of all social relations, everlasting uncertainty and agitation, distinguish the bourgeois epoch from all earlier times."

He waved the book at me like a flag. "Do you know what that means for a writer?"

"It sounds—"

Schmuck! If I was going to be a Bixby-born writer I should learn to recognize a rhetorical question when I heard one. Bixby poured on.

"Get this: *All fixed, fast-frozen relationships, with their train of venerable ideas and opinions, are swept away, all new-formed ones become obsolete before they can ossify.*

"And here's the kicker. *All that is solid melts into air, all that is holy is profaned, and men at last are forced to face with sober senses the real conditions of their lives and their relations with their fellow men.*

"Look how exciting Marx makes the bourgeois period. UNREALITY, my ass. All that is solid melts into air, all that is holy is profaned. . . ."

"Then you think I should read Marx—"

"God, no." He tossed the little book at me. I shoved it

into my pocket like an obedient student. "You'll probably get stuck on the Labor Theory of Value and Hegelian dialectics. Worst thing in the world for you at this stage. I want you to hear their mysterious song. Understand?"

I did not, of course, in any conventional way. But I was learning from Bixby the way youth learns best—by the communicated passion and person of the teacher. "There was a touch in your story, yesterday. The part where the man dies in the synagogue, killed by prayers. That fantasy moment is your key."

Such enthusiasm was impossible to fight. I must not, however, Bixby warned me, go commercial. Most of sci-fi was junk. BEMs (Bug-Eyed Monsters) and Space Opera. I must read Arthur C. Clarke, a young writer named Ray Bradbury, the books of Charles Fort. The glorious conversation climaxed with an offer to submit my story to *Cosmos* for publication. Then Bixby asked if he could return twelve of the eighteen dollars he'd borrowed the day before and owe me six. The modern artist, he added, as he handed me the ten-dollar bill and two singles, is the first ever to have to create from his own insides. The center does not hold, no foundation all the way down the line. What the artist needed to survive in addition to silence, exile, and cunning was a direct line to this time. That line was to be fantasy and science fiction. And the best-kept secret of our day was that Karl Marx was one of the great modernists along with Joyce, Proust, and Valéry. I had read neither Yeats nor Saroyan, neither Joyce nor Marx, so I got none of his references. I simply nodded and went home to type up my story for editorial submission and to think about silence, exile, cunning, and art, none of which I had thought much about before. It seemed to me, though, as if I had been secretly thinking these thoughts for years. It may have been truth or it may have been the music of Bixby's passion. To dwell on that at the moment seemed to me to be missing the point.

Lying in bed that night I opened the beat-up *Manifesto* at random. I read: *Modern bourgeois society, a society that has conjured up such mighty means of production and exchange, is like the sorcerer who can no longer control the powers of the underworld that he has called up by his spells.*

I felt my skin ripple with eerie anxiety. Perhaps because Bixby had told me, specifically, not to read what I had just read. Or perhaps it was the Frankensteinian imagery. The whole question of "productivity" was a family mystery. In the Vienna from which my parents had come anyone with enough nerve, luck, and some relatives to supply capital could do well in a small business: jewelry, factoring (the lending of money to textile manufacturers to get through a season)—anything. When they got to America this family was crazy enough to ignore the postwar phenomenon of the college education. With the exception of my older brother, who went to medical school, everyone else seemed to be floating around in a vague soup of small business hopes. Petit-bourgeois indeed.

It's difficult to express the particular sort of cultural / money mixture that makes up a certain kind of second-generation family life. Perhaps it was only my special family-plant which flourished on Mosholu Parkway in the Bronx. Daily life seemed to be all about values: education, decency, old-fashioned, traditional liberal Jewish politics . . . but the latent content, the substructure, was an immense, all-pervading anxiety, a rage, about and for money.

Don't get the wrong idea—there wasn't any money around, at least not at first. But in the unreal life of the Anxiety of Affluence, a ten-dollar bill will stand in perfectly well for ten thousand-dollar bills. My grandmother taught herself to read English by reading the Scott Moncrieff translation of Proust. Eccentric but admirable in a seventy-year-old Austrian refugee. Yet, when my father wished to restart his career as a businessman all over again, in America—retail jewelry—she loaned him the starting money at the prevailing interest rate, prime plus two points. More like Balzac than Proust, you might say. But sensibility was sensibility and money was money: as simple as that.

Not so simple to me. When it filtered down to me, the whole question of money had an eerie aura about it. *Money.* . . . The word spoken or implied had deep reservoirs of unspoken power—and along with it, danger. This may have been connected with an extraordinary incident involving my father's younger brother, Irving.

My family had specialized in an exquisite confusion of values. Study the violin, read books, learn, and above all make a good living, marry, and raise a family. Art, culture, money, and family were what life was all about. All unspoken but clear. Clear as mud—so I dismissed them all by age fourteen. The exception was my Uncle Irving, the outlaw Voltaire, the Thomas Mann of Attorney Street, to whom employment did not come naturally, the black sheep of the family, who had devised a sort of personal extralegal aesthetic and economic philosophy.

"Look, kid," he said. "Nobody owns nothing. Everybody is born—they grow up, they walk down the streets of the world and they see buildings, stores, cars, barrels, trucks, signs, sometimes farms or mountainsides, and, since you're human, it all seems to belong to you. Even if it did—which it probably doesn't—you're going to die sooner or later—probably sooner—and then it's not going to belong to you *again!* So the trick is: *act as if it does! Use the illusion!* People only have to believe you for a little while, if your luck holds out. This, my boy, is as true for the average American Jew as it was for J. P. Morgan or Jenny Grossinger. At the start, anyway."

So much for theory. But my Uncle Irving believed in the Unity of Theory and Practice as much as any orthodox Marxist. (You understand, I knew none of these slick left-wing terms at the time. I learned them later when Manishin made it a condition of our continuing courtship for me to attend the Jefferson School, formerly the Workers School, on East Sixteenth Street.) What Uncle Irving did next was exemplary. He was the manager of a cigar store—retail sales being the only refuge of the willfully uneducated. He bet the store on the World Series— and lost. This would not have been as bad as it turned out, except for the fact that he did not *own* the cigar store, he'd only *acted* as if he'd owned it. Consistent, my Uncle Irving, as perhaps no philosopher has been before or since.

And some people, professional gamblers, had believed him for the little while he'd asked. But not long enough. The men he'd bet with did not have a philosophic turn of mind. They called on my father to find out where his brother was hiding.

"Forget it," my father said. "He hasn't got a dime."

"We know," one of them with a sense of humor said. "The dime he doesn't have is ours."

"Look," another one said. "He bets with us and wins for months. The first time he loses he cops a big one— and he welches."

"He got overconfident," my father said. "He's an immigrant like me, an idealist. Couldn't believe the Brooklyn Dodgers could lose."

"He told us he owned the store. Some idealist?"

"He'd like to own it," my father explained patiently. "That's what idealism is, as opposed to materialism, where you *really* own it. He'd run it better, too, believe me."

"Look, we don't want to kill anybody. Maybe just work him over a little. A lesson to others. That's a promise."

I recall my father's fine moment of dignity. He stood slowly, at the rickety kitchen table, and placed his hands before him, flat down, like a lawyer.

"I have a photographic memory," he said carefully. "One hand on him and you're all in jail."

When Irving returned from exile in New Jersey, months later, I told him some of the highlights of the conversation. He seized, at first, on what I thought was an odd, minor point.

"Your dad was right," he said. "That *should* have been my store. A great location and Greenblatt does nothing with it. No in-store promotion, no outdoor advertising. Just waits for people to come by for a cigar, a pack of cigarettes, a Zippo lighter. I tell you, if I'd won, I would have bought the place from Greenblatt and turned it into a winner."

"But it wasn't yours," I said, stupid with literal morality. "How could you bet it as if you owned it?"

Instead of getting angry, Irving reached over and hugged me. He was skinny and bony, a little like Bixby. All the people who have exhorted me about life, over the years, have been like skeletons, for some reason.

"It's a comfort, kid. A great comfort. I mean, you appropriate something for yourself, from all the things in the world around you—you pick something and you say—mine! Even if it doesn't finally work out—it makes you feel less helpless. Babies don't know any better and they do it, right? Mine, mine. . . . And maybe nobody should. But it's a torment—a world full of money and music and women and vicuña jackets and foreign cars. Your average person has to do *something* to feel better. Do you understand that?"

I hadn't. But I tried to now, faced with the new electricity of Bixby's injunction to use my family's cash-craziness. *All that is solid melts into air.* . . . I began to sketch out a story, something growing out of Irving and his special approach to private property. As for myself, I had neither money nor cashmere jackets nor cars—my only music came from Bixby and his Scriabin-piano and my woman was a somewhat unsatisfactory young Army officer I'd picked up in Central Park during a rainstorm.

In those days my connections with women seemed to have a built-in time limit. Some would burst brightly in less than a month, for nonreasons: temperament, sudden travel arrangements, entropy. Others would gradually develop cracks and flaws based on "real" differences and dissolve in nine months or less. Those seemed to be the magic numbers: one month or nine. It rarely troubled me. Love was not covered by the G.I. Bill.

That night I lay in bed next to the current connection, Marie Sullivan, a recently discharged WAC who spoke in her sleep all night; spoke in some indecipherable tongue. While she spoke I turned over what Bixby had said. I remembered my Uncle Irving and his bony hungry smile. The next day after typing up my story and mailing it to *Cosmos*, I sat down to write a new story for that week's class. Strange images were sucked from my typewriter's keys onto the paper. My imagination seemed to come from someone else. Odder than Scriabin in waltz time, a story shaped itself in less than a day. Based on Irving the outcast, it exalted him as the metaphysical outsider, ennobled his passion for gambling, and sang a sweet mystical song of criminality. When I read it to the class I was astonished when, at the end, there was a pause, then a smack of applause cracked the air. That finished me off. Or, rather, started me off. For the next six months I swam in a sea of productivity, with Bixby at my side. *Cosmos* rejected the first story but by the time I received the form letter it touched me not at all. I was already deep into Joyce, Flaubert, H. G. Wells, Wilkie Collins, Henry James, and Mme. Blavatsky. The mixture of great moderns and trash mysticism was just right for my unravished mind and new talents.

In the meantime Bixby kept touching me for modest, odd-numbered sums of money, none of which ever quite got paid back. Tight as I was for cash, as we all were in those days, it seemed a small price to pay for Bixby's infusion of energy and point into my life. I began sending stories out to the little magazines. Needing more sleep for this energetic new life, I moved out of Marie Sullivan's apartment; her sleep-talking tolled my sleep too much. Besides, by this time Bixby had her into Dianetics and there were meetings in the apartment at all hours when I wanted to work. Bixby was living there too, having as it turned out no fixed home of his own.

"Bixby is for fun, for listening to at the piano. But you have to admit he's weird." Mettro had doubts. I admitted nothing. Fond of Mettro as I was, I had doubts about *him.* His Public Relations education had already yielded some free-lance jobs. Khaki pants had given way to slacks and sport coats. There was a lot less talk about Paris. The Gauloises had given way to Pall Malls. Mettro had always been my connection to reality. After all, anybody who could take apart a car and put it back together again had to be in touch with things as they are. If there was a point to Mettro it was a kind of easygoing practicality to daily life. But Mettro's point had collided with Bixby's, somewhere in my floating soul of the time. For the moment Bixby's point was sharper, though Mettro's impinged more each day. For one thing, I was being thrown out of the Art Students League for demonstrable lack of talent, as well as absenteeism, which reached a new high post-Bixby. For another, I had only one more year left on the G.I.

Bill. Mettro's reality would soon be breathing hard on the neck of Bixby's imagination. So much for Bixby and Mettro. It is time for Manishin.

Here is Manishin greeting us at the door at 8:15 P.M. on Wednesday, April 23, 1948. She is quite small, looks up at me and Mettro, the whole top part of her drenched in long, red hair. Beneath all the hair you could see a kind of Mexican patterned shawl and a determined smile.

"Hey, I'm Manishin," she said. "The game hasn't started yet."

Ah, Manishin, Barbara Manishin, hippie and feminist before your time, Beat Generation twenty years too early, smoker of marijuana when it was still called tea and Mary Jane, raiser of two daughters according to the principles of George Bernard Shaw, the game had indeed just started; the longest game either of us would ever play. While Mettro helped Bixby and a few others set up the chips in neat piles on the table—I suddenly had an inkling as to where those peculiar sums of money Bixby had been borrowing for months had gone—Manishin and I spoke. It was one of those first conversations that happen, I think, only in New York. Intimacies and epiphanies tumbled over each other in the first rush of realizing we found each other interesting, or at least attractive. Questions brought answers not evasions; statements brought surprises.

"Why do you call yourself Manishin—your last name."

"Hey," she said. Manishin seemed to enjoy getting your attention with that silly word. "Hey, it's my father's name. Women are given women's names to keep them in their place. I haven't decided my place yet so I'm Manishin not Barbara. What do you do?"

"I'm a writer."

I'd never said that before. It startled the hell out of me. So much so, in fact, that I poured out Bixby's dream of revitalizing the modern tradition by the Marxist magic of fantasy and science fiction.

"Yes," Manishin said. "I know all about it."

"You do?"

"Sure. Bixby sings beautiful songs. I like him."

"Do you—are you—have you?" I stumbled.

"Not anymore. We tried it. Then I got married to a nice man—turned out to be a forger. I have two daughters and I'm going to Columbia Law School. Want a toke? It's good tea. How about you and women? What goes?"

Her abruptness compelled some kind of honesty. I told her all the fragments of my fragmentary life with women for the last two years. I told her the peculiar development of each affair—the gradual involvement, the movement towards intimacy, the dropping of the guard, the slow moving in of shirts, underwear, records, books; then traced the beginning of each provocation in a variety of shapes and sizes.

Lilla, the redheaded Quaker girl who spent Saturdays and Sundays copying Caravaggios at the Metropolitan Museum and all week long was an executive secretary in Wall Street. I borrowed three hundred dollars from her, seriously questioned Quakerism as religious thought, and never returned the money—until after she'd sent me packing.

I told her of Jamie, the lovely Pre-Raphaelite actress who wanted to marry me and have children at once . . . and how I teased her with promises of reform, of getting out of bed early in the morning . . . of getting a job, renting an apartment, opening an account with the New York Telephone Company; promises all welshed on as Jamie's delicate features, her soft gray eyes and light-line mouth, grew weary and finally bitter. Then, one day, she vanished with a road company of *Saint Joan* and left me alone once again.

All these fragments poured out to Manishin. She nodded her small, oval, red-haired noggin wisely and smiled that knowing smile women have when they see a point you have not yet seen.

The cards might have been Tarot cards for all the sense I could make out of them that night. I was entirely enchanted by the red-haired elf who counted out her chips and, businesslike, plunged into poker, dealing, raising, bluffing. For many months I had allowed women as little time and attention as possible. I had preferred their conversation to be on the order of Marie Sullivan's—my sleep-talking former soldier. Now, instead of counting my cards I was counting the minutes, the hours, until I could walk Manishin home.

All of the players appeared to be science fiction writers, editors, and patients or practitioners of Dianetics as well as Marxists of one persuasion or another—often not clear which—a poker game as much a scrimmage of beliefs as it was of chance and bluff. It was one of those evenings that burned itself up in the energies and conflicts of the players. Prickly, edgy, competitive—like the

science students I'd known in high school—they badg-
ered and bit at each other's styles and souls until an
eruption was inevitable.

The fight, itself, when it came, started because someone accused the host of cutting the pot for more money
than was needed to pay for the sandwiches and coffee.
From there it moved to angry ideological small talk. The
small talk became shouts and the shouts became fists with
astonishing speed.

"Twenty bucks for seven sandwiches?"

"It's my apartment. I maintain it. That takes money
and work. So I get an extra cut. It's the Labor Theory of
Value."

"It's sophistry, otherwise known as bullshit. If you're
basing the extra cut on landownership, you're talking
Henry George and the Single Tax theory. This is the kind
of doubletalk they dished out at the Moscow Trials."

"The Moscow Trials were necessary to cleanse the
Revolution."

"Cleanse? They were filthy setups. How can you defend
them?"

"Those guys—Bukharin and Zinoviev had to be guilty.
Otherwise, why didn't they defend themselves?"

"Don't ask me. Read *Darkness at Noon.*"

"The pot's light. Somebody didn't ante."

"Not me. And how can you defend Stalin—betrayer of
Communism?"

"Who's to say what Communism really is?"

"It's been said. 'Soviet Power Plus Rural Electrifica-
tion Equal Communism.' "

"I can't believe you said that."

"I didn't. Lenin did."

"I raise."

"You can't! There's a limit. Three raises."

"A bourgeois convention. See my raise or get out!"

"Get out? I'll throw *you* out first!"

Chips started to fly, chairs were turned over. It was the Marxist New York version of a western. Before anybody could shoot out the lights, Bixby appeared at my elbow, eyes wide with revelation.

"You see," he said. "This is what I warned you about." He ducked to avoid a stream of chips followed by a shower of pastrami.

"Listen," he said, "you don't belong with these people." He seemed to have forgotten that I was there at his invitation. "This is what their so-called revolutionary imaginations come down to—this earthbound Socialism. Go home and write. Create a Socialism of the Imagination. MAKE IT NEW!" With that he threw himself into the fight with a fine Welsh-Indian rage and Manishin, Mettro, and I fled.

My God! No one had ever said "Make it new" to me before that moment. And since Ezra Pound had not been invited to my bar mitzvah, there was no way for me to know that Bixby was, to put it kindly, "adapting." It didn't matter. Bixby was bringing me the news of the twentieth century—and if it was coming late in the game, it was certainly at the beginning of *my* game.

We left Mettro at the Sheridan Square subway station and walked west to Hudson Street, where Manishin lived. We exchanged lives, as young people do on such impromptu occasions. I remember nothing of all she told me—and we stayed up talking until the morning tugs hooted into the Hudson dawn—except for one tale. She told me of her grandmother in Odessa—a ferocious revolutionary in her heart—Manishin's model. She'd joined every subterranean organization for change she could find—while bearing eight children; seven boys and one golden girl. One Friday afternoon she'd rushed home from a secret political meeting, in a desperate hurry to prepare the Sabbath meal in time for sundown. It was May and her four-year-old golden girl was playing with her playmates; there was a Maypole and she had been Queen of the May. Then, flushed with excitement, she ran home. Her mother was sitting in the kitchen peeling potatoes. The little girl ran up to her, her face covered with a fine dew of perspiration; she was happily out of breath. Then, a smile of delight on her face, she laid her small head on her mother's lap—and died.

Manishin told it to me in wonder. One moment alive, Queen-of-the-May young; the next moment gone, her head on her mother's unsuspecting lap. She even shaped the tale for me as she told it: the awful intrusion of irrational death into rational political life.

"Engels breaks your heart writing about the exploitation of working-class children in the industrial nations," she said. "They die awful, early deaths, too. But this was full of extra mystery." In a thousand years, Manishin mused, sadly, after we've won all the battles, after each person is giving according to his abilities and each is receiving according to his needs—a child could still come back to her mother's lap to rest from play—and die.

"Hey," she said, trying to break the mood, "that's no excuse for child labor. It's just some extra mystery."

I walked home that morning, balancing this delicate tale on one hand and Bixby's mad admonition on the other. Politics and fantasy. I wrote the story in two days and I knew as I wrote it that it would change my life one way or another. I knew Bixby would be delighted with it. But when I searched him out to show it to him, he was gone. My former night-talker Marie told me he'd split for the Coast.

"He owes me three hundred and sixty dollars," she said. "Your friend."

"Don't blame him on me," I said. "Besides, he owes me a hundred and eighty."

"Why does he always ask for these odd numbers?"

"Damned if I know."

"Listen," Marie said. "It's lonely here now. Do you want to stay over?"

"I can't," I said, though I could have, and instead went over to Mettro's place. I had a hunch I might find Bixby there. Somehow in those young days everyone's place seemed to be for friends, acquaintances, encounters, even friends of friends, to hole up in. The grown-up bourgeois notion of your "home" as exclusive rather than inclusive came much later. But, given that atmosphere, even so Bixby was running out of places to shack up. Mettro might be the last. I'd guessed right. Bixby was there (Mettro wasn't)—and he was packing.

"What's up?" I asked.

"I'm getting out of here."

"To where?"

"The Coast."

I sat down, as confused as the sprawl of luggage on the bed.

"Why west?"

"Because the east is played out." As always Bixby spoke in prophetic tones.

"But how about the life you've gotten me into?"

Bixby stopped packing the pounds of khaki underwear (he had actually been folding khaki handkerchiefs). "Time, please," he muttered. "It's time," wasting his quotation on me, who had never played darts in an English pub and had not read *The Waste Land*. Both of which, of course, Bixby had triumphantly done. And for the next ten minutes I tried to decipher the lyrics of Bixby's departure-song.

It was time apparently for me to give up the fantasy motif and recognize the secret of my family's dirty little secret: what Marx called "the callous cash nexus." The story about my Uncle Irving and the betting of the cigar store he did not own had made an impression—even though *Cosmos* had turned it down. It was time for me to recognize the criminality of the petty bourgeoisie which was my family's legacy.

"Your big temptation is going to be the cash nexus. Fight it! You could be the first real Marxist Modernist. But it means you may have to learn to eat rocks. The bourgeois culture is not going to reward you with money, for trying to replace it with something better. Don't listen to Mettro."

"He hasn't said a word."

"Wait! He's developing a revisionist theory of the *Manifesto.*"

"I thought he was getting into public relations."

"Both! They will intersect, soon. The trick is for you not to be standing exactly where they meet. It's all going to be about money. Hold fast!"

"Are you giving up the struggle?"

He stopped packing and sat down next to me.

"I need sunshine, the doctor says. I have diabetes."

The connection between a sugar and insulin imbalance and the California sun escaped me. I didn't press it.

"Do you remember what I told you about—"

"Yes?"

"About how I couldn't—you know—have sex?"

"I heard, I forget from who. But Manishin said that you and she—"

"Manishin," Bixby said, "was a misunderstanding. We both tried hard to penetrate and we were both afraid to yield so it all got mixed up and we didn't know who should do what to whom or how. . ."

"Sounds a mess."

"Was a mess. But that was before she married her *gonif* and started a new life." I was feeling something unpleasant in my stomach, my place where jealousy has always lodged. It was a strong, painful sensation. But not strong enough to erase my identity as the eternally agreeable, ambitious acolyte, "Okay," I said. "But you haven't read this new story."

Bixby paused to pop a handful of vitamins past the important presence of his Adam's apple.

"Listen," he said. "Can you lend me ninety dollars?" I did some fast figuring. That would leave me about thirty dollars till the end of the month. I was helpless before Bixby. But I also couldn't resist asking him the basis for the odd needs that always seemed to require sums divisible by eighteen.

"Didn't I tell you?" he said as he folded the check into his shirt pocket. "That my grandmother was Jewish and eighteen is the numerical equivalent for life: *chai?* A sacred number."

"Welsh, you said your grandmother was Welsh."

I was growing panicky dealing with a vanishing Bixby. He seemed to be growing less substantial every minute, both in the present and in his past history. He had never carved out much air and space for the eyes to hold on to. Which may have been why it was so important to me that his history should hold up under scrutiny. Bixby, a skinny dancer-on-air, player of Scriabin siren-songs on his piano and on my needy imagination.

"Oh." He smiled a thin khaki-smile. "That was my other grandmother."

"She was Indian, you said."

He snapped the suitcase shut and sat down, suddenly.

"My father's father married a lot of women. I didn't know them all. But one of them was Jewish. Anyway, I'm good and scared."

Fear and Bixby; an impossible combination! He was the Fred Astaire, the Simon Templar, of combined commitment and insouciance. It turned out that what he was terrified of was flying. So much for the Air Force officer's cap he'd rakishly sported since we'd met. These contradictions, these strands of not-quite-truths or imagined truths gleaming in the midst of Bixby's quotidian Marxist ordinary truth, did not throw me. Was he a part-Jew who had slept with my night-talking WAC, Marie, as well as my past, present, and future Manishin, or was he an impotent Welsh-Indian, self-taught pianist with a knack for science fiction, a passion for a mysterious brand of his own literary Marxist modernism, and a flying phobia? Did anyone in their youth have a more comic-book Master?

Bixby, creator of an impossible socialism, is going to California to dream.

I left him sitting amid luggage and anxieties with a copy of my story in his hand. From a street phone I called Manishin and arranged to be invited over for a drink— or as it turned out, to begin the second installment of what was to be an endless courtship.

I picked up a bottle of Polish vodka with a spear of buffalo grass in it—my only addiction. It was one hundred proof. I wasn't sure if the extra proof was for me or for Manishin.

"The last time I was here the poker got pretty intense."

"Hey, that wasn't poker. That was ideology."

"Tough game. It's harder to tell who wins and who loses."

"Easier to cheat at, too. Thanks for this vodka. It tastes weird but nice."

"It's the grass, I think. And maybe some chemicals."

She was dressed in various shades of red and her red

hair, I now saw, came down to her waist. There were flowering plants and ivy everywhere. I'd never seen so many plants outside of a greenhouse where I once had a summer job.

I came right out with what was on my mind. Either because I was falling in love or because I was young.

"I just saw Bixby. You and he were a big thing, right?"

"Wrong."

"Aha."

"Bixby is Fantasy, I'm Science Fiction. You can't have a big thing with a Fantasy."

"Not to mention his famous organ problem."

"Yes—I would say not to mention that."

"Discretion? Delicacy?"

"Maybe it's Fantasy . . ."

"He's vanishing. I just saw him."

"I know. A restless soul."

"Listen, we stayed up all night, you and me—after that crazy poker game."

"You and I."

"The two of us."

She swigged some of the greenish vodka and said: "I'm going to Columbia Law School. I'm preparing myself to be very precise. I'm going to be a judge, someday. A judge has to be very precise."

"When was the last time you stayed up all night with somebody?"

"Hey," she said. "Hey. You're stuck in a groove! Jealousy is just a claiming of private property. Even an ordinary, everyday capitalist knows you have to acquire the property first. You going to be jealous of Bixby and every other man I ever went with—at this stage? Why don't you just kiss me, first. Let's do things in order!"

Great idea! It was one of those first kisses that come loaded with promise. I mean it felt like a thousandth kiss. When we started gasping for oxygen, Manishin reached up and pulled her red shift over her head.

And that's not what astonished me. Not just her apparent willingness. What got to me was: she was NAKED. She'd been sitting there, a Columbia Law School student, independent mother of two little girls, wearing no underwear, in 1949. In the days and months to come, Manishin was to make a hundred, a thousand political statements about men, women, private property, freedom, and the Origins of the Family, Private Property, and the State. But none of it equaled the pure political intensity of pulling that red cotton sheath over her head, to reveal that slender, boyish body, cuplike breasts with tiny dark-red aureoles prickly with the flow of air or desire. And after our first kiss!

"I want to marry you," I murmured.

"Why? Because we stayed up all night, talking?"

"Because we're perfect together."

"As simple as that?" She had not stopped kissing me since I'd asked her to marry me. I was standing there fully dressed, she was naked. It was weird. But not as weird as what happened next. She grabbed my hand and pulled me into the adjoining room. Books cluttered the floor, the walls, a desk in the corner facing the summer buzz of Second Avenue.

Manishin ran along the wall running her hand across the spines of books until she found the one she wanted.

More naked waiting—shuffling and thumbing of pages and then: aha! She read, in her loud clear Manishin-voice:

"Although romantic idealists generally insist on self-surrender as an indispensable element in true womanly love . . ."

"Hey," I said, borrowing her favorite expletive, "what is that book? I never said anything about surrender . . ."

Like all smart teachers, dressed or undressed, she knew enough to ignore student interruptions.

". . . its repulsive effect is well known and feared in practice by both sexes . . ."

"What . . . ?"

"Love loses its charm when it is not free; and whether the compulsion is that of custom and law, or of infatuation, the effect is the same. . . . Here"—she gestured the book at me like a conductor's baton—"he says—*it becomes valueless and even abhorrent, like the caresses of a maniac . . ."*

In a matter of moments I'd gone from being a welcomed present or future lover to a caressing maniac. Who was this son of a bitch she was reading to me? I tried to grab the book to see, but she danced away. Some of her long, bright red hair trailed over the page and she flipped it off, impatiently, over her shoulder.

"Here it is," she said. "Here: *the intense repugnance inspired by the compulsory character of the legalized conjugal relation that leads, first to the idealization of marriage whilst it remains indispensable as a means of perpetuating society; then to its modification by divorce . . ."*

I got hold of the book. "Whilst?" was all I could think

of to complain about. "What writer uses a word like 'whilst'?" She had the book back in a second. It was clear who was in charge.

You'd think I would have taken offense at the mention of divorce only a few undressed minutes after our first kiss and my proposal of marriage. But, no, all I could think of was the damned foreign-sounding foolishness of "whilst."

"It's British for 'while,' " she said. "This is George Bernard Shaw. My hero. Look how he finishes off the idea of marriage with a metaphor: *Marriage is thus, by force of circumstances, compelled to buy extension of life by extension of divorce, much as if a fugitive should try to delay a pursuing wolf by throwing portions of his own heart to it.*"

"Isn't that beautiful—a kind of Marxian poetry."

She tossed the book at me. It smelled of her perfume, now; something very light and flowery; very Manishin. The book was *The Quintessence of Ibsenism.* I wonder if I was to have it to keep and put beside Bixby's copy of *The Communist Manifesto.*

"He makes the same point in *Major Barbara,*" Manishin said. "I'll take you to see the movie. Rex Harrison is wonderful."

"If you want me to stop asking you to marry me, you'd better lend me the book. And don't tell me how wonderful other men are."

"Take it," she said, putting her arms around me. "I don't believe in private property anyway."

We collapsed into an even longer kiss than the first.

"You know, we're in the bedroom," she said. She kicked the couch next to us. "This opens up."

Suddenly nervous, I said: "Where are the kids?"

"Trotskyite sleepaway camp. Two weeks."

I began to fumble with furniture and while I was pulling I said, "What pushed you to where you are? How'd you get to all this politics about men and marriage?"

"I was so miserable being married. When you're that miserable you weep and weep—and when your eyes calm down and clear up, you read. A friend gave me a pamphlet called 'Lenin on the Woman Question.' By the time I was divorced, I'd worn out three hardcover copies."

"Listen," I said. "Forget Lenin, forget George Bernard Shaw, Manishin. Marry me."

"I'd rather die," Manishin said, kissing me passionately and struggling with the knot in my tie at the same time.

It seemed she instinctively knew the point of my amorous vita interrupta with all the women in my postwar life. A point which, if it existed, I had missed thus far. But, like all good analysts, like all good prophets, she taught only by indirection, by example. Her method, in my case, consisted of loving me very calmly, studying carefully for her Law Boards, making no demands, lending me no money,and refusing to respond to any provocations. Nothing I did could make her either leave me or marry me. It was maddening! She was entirely—in the early fifties, imagine—her own woman. And she insisted that I be my own man. It was no use my telling her that parallel lines meet only in infinity. That was an old wives' tale. Parallel lives, she said, were the only ones that could meet in the present. So, I made my own way in the present the best way I could.

I wrote stories, I planned novels, I read the peculiar mixture of great modernists and questionable freaks that constitute the influences prescribed by the vanished Bixby. (I'd learned from the G.I. Bill grapevine that Bixby had actually fled to the Coast chased by an angry husband who refused to believe his tales of impotence.) In any case, his exhortations of me had "taken" like an injection of some magical elixir. The story of the Queen of the May was accepted by *The New Yorker*. I stopped drawing; I stopped dancing. To hell with the G.I. Bill. I was a Writer! Obeying the prophet of Scriabin, I did not squabble over pennies: I wrote. I saw few pennies. The *New Yorker* publication was the first and last sale. The rest of the stories I wrote were given away, mostly to magazines bearing the names of states or localities; the *Colorado Quarterly* cherished my work; the *Southern Review* allowed me below the Mason-Dixon literary line; the *Antioch Review* paid me in copies of the magazine. Nevertheless, I was talked about sometimes in oddly Bixbyish terms; one article mentioned me as a link between the early English line of fantasy and the modernist movement. Heady stuff like that. Interestingly, Marx was never mentioned.

Until I showed up on Mettro's doorstep, one early spring evening (is it my imagination or was my youth entirely composed of spring and summer evenings?), to touch the most successful member of our little band for a loan. It was the second anniversary of my first meeting with Manishin and a celebration was indicated—but the means were not.

I explained this to Mettro, who was most understanding.

"It was only a question of time," he said, ladling out the cost of dinner for two at a Village restaurant and maybe a cab home, afterwards, mostly in singles—a heavy wad.

"What do you mean?"

"I mean you've been a prisoner of Bixby's romanticism for long enough." He had forked over the money and was now shining his shoes; Mettro, the only shiner of shoes or, indeed, wearer of shined shoes I can remember from that unshiny time.

"A voluntary prisoner," I said, defending Bixby by defending myself. "And pretty productive."

"Marx said"—the first time I'd heard the name fall from Mettro's lips—"that Bixby's beloved bourgeoisie had a special genius for wringing the profit out of thinkers and artists. Well, where's your profit?" Before I could perform one of my specialties, which was the answering of rhetorical questions, he held up his hand. "No mystery," he said. "You've just been ignoring the one form created by and for the bourgeoisie: *the novel.*"

"I've been writing short stories."

"Right. For elegant little nonpaying magazines. Besides, your kind of literary modern short story is an expressive device, the novel in the marketplace is a fungible artifact. That means it can be an effective medium of exchange.

. . . The cash nexus—don't be a schmuck—it goes for art the same as for industrial enterprises."

"Will I find that in *The Communist Manifesto?*"

"Look at that shine," Mettro said. "It's like a mirror. You can see your face in it."

I took this to mean no. Bixby's warning that Mettro was preparing a cash-rich revisionist theory had been right on the button.

Which would have cooled me off on Mettro except that he had apparently read my story about Irving the Outcast; not only had read it but thought it would make a novel that would sell. The trick about any era, Mettro said, the bourgeois one included, was to survive it.

Crammed with pasta, overflowing with wine and love and lust for Manishin, after our Mettro-financed anniversary celebration, I returned to my typewriter and began my novel: *The Doctor Faustus of Rivington Street.* It took me seven months to turn a tense, ironic short story into a sprawling Lower East Side novel with demonic overtones. Mettro introduced me to Martha Maxwell, a sharp-tongued, sharp-suited young woman who was an editor at Random House. I thought she might be a Lesbian. But I was on guard against received ideas—and she might simply have been the first young businesswoman I ever saw who wore a different suit each time we met.

"I love the manuscript," she said. "It needs work—but I think it is just the answer to the pseudo-moralities which are flooding the marketplace, after the recent unpleasantness [that's the war—a joke—Ha, I said]. Everybody has a moral or political philosophy to sell, except your character Oscar [read Irving. I'd naturally changed the name to protect the guilty]. He's the only man in contemporary literature who has a kind of ontological approach to Making It. Betting that cigar store is like Gide's Gratuitous Act in *The Counterfeiters*. Have you read *The Counterfeiters?*"

"No," I said. "Will my book sell?" I asked.

"If I have anything to say about it, it will," said Martha the Mouth, as Mettro called her. I assumed he was referring to her verbal energies. Astonishingly, Random House put their money where Martha's mouth was. They accepted the novel and paid me two thousand dollars as an advance. I was in the world, at last.

But disaster and disappointment led the way to publication. Halfway through, Martha Maxwell quit to go to McGraw-Hill and nobody at the publishers seemed to know who or what I was, after that. The reviews were amazing. They understood me perfectly. I was invited to live and write at a writers' colony on the West Coast. Only the sales failed to arrive. Three thousand copies. I was left owing the publisher about a thousand dollars. Thus I was slightly lower on the cash nexus scale than I'd been before.

Mettro's revisionist theory had failed me—or I had failed it; it was not clear which.

While this was going on I pursued Manishin in and out of bed, into dreams of permanence and on into frustration. She loved me but was having none of it. Marriage, she chanted, was the end of friendship. Permanence was a confession of the failure of individual moments. It was useless for me to complain that witty, depressing epigrams were no substitute for happiness. If she wanted to put an end to one or another of my campaigns, Manishin had only to point out that rebuilding the modern tradition in literature boiled no pots, fed no children. (Though she was by this time clerking for a judge in Brooklyn and could look forward to a good salary as a lawyer.)

"If men shouldn't support women anymore, neither should women make children out of men by supporting them." She had more theories than I had strength.

"Furthermore," she added, "I have two kids in private school."

"And if I *could* support them . . . ?"

"It wouldn't make marriage less of a master/slave relationship. We're alert to each other, physically and emotionally. It's terrific! We have everything husbands and wives have except the detachment that comes from constant exposure, and my taking care of your laundry."

"Is that Shaw again?" I sniffed a point I was only partially getting.

"Partly," Manishin said.

"I can't stand this," I said. "The other man in my life is in his nineties and has a bushy beard."

I gave up for the moment and followed Bixby to the Coast. I carried with me my Bixby-born seriousness of purpose, my noisy silence, my portable exile, and my financial cunning to a writer's colony in the Pacific Palisades Mountains; scattered cottages, rolling lawns, a swimming pool, and hot noons as still as graveyards.

It was a paradise of sorts; one of those places run by a foundation and established by somebody who, in his lifetime, worshiped art and the artist. Such philanthropists are superb artists at Missing the Point. By setting up sylvan retreats where writers will be entirely undisturbed they exquisitely miss the point that writers wish for nothing so much as to be disturbed. Of course they also want the food and shelter such places contribute. But they would much rather have it sent to them in the form of cash at their home address. However, since the terms of the will were otherwise, I went west. I had no idea where Bixby was. Mettro had joined the West Coast exodus a year before. Southern California, he'd told me as farewell, is the Fatherland of Public Relations. The slacks and sport coats that had replaced army surplus khaki pants had given way to three-button gray suits. The forties were over. The fifties had arrived.

I was restless in Paradise. I could not concentrate on my third novel. Five thousand dollars in debt, two rejected novels, and a tiny, redheaded beauty who would sleep with me but would not marry me. I did not yet know that I might be missing the point; or, in fact, what the point might be to each of the recent movements I had made, either complete or abortive. Surrounded by the bald and foolish palm trees of Southern California, I pondered the sheer Americanness of what I'd been doing—to listen to outside voices. Thus, I had listened to Bixby's voice and taken up the flowering pen of Joyce and Pound and vows of modernist poverty; had listened to Manishin, had stayed (reluctantly) free and single.

Mettro arrived one day for a visit driving a stripped-down lean animal of a Maserati with an Alfa Romeo engine he had installed himself, piece by piece. We sat by the pool and shared my box lunch. I wore a bathing suit, Mettro wore a three-button gray silk suit. I sweated. He did not. The crickets stitched the only sounds; the noon heat congealed around us like invisible cream. Mettro said, "This place is marvelous. So isolated. It makes me nervous. But I'm not an artist."

I said, "It makes me nervous, too. Yet there are people who go from one of these places to another all year, every year."

"How are you and Manishin doing?"

"Fine, except she won't marry me."

"Is it money?"

"It's confused. Independence, friendship-preservation. She reads a lot of Shaw. I don't know."

"It's always money. I read that novel about your Uncle Albert . . ."

"Irving . . ."

"The Spinoza of Houston Street . . ."

"The Doctor Faustus of Rivington Street. Close enough."

"It was good. It had balls. Bixby lent me his copy."

"Bixby? You see him?"

"Bixby," Mettro said, "is a will-o'-the-wisp. He has abandoned Scriabin and Marxism. It's Romanticism, now—the English Romantics—Vaughan Williams, William Walton . . . He is also apparently involved in a nonstop high-stakes poker game he cannot afford. He owes me eighteen hundred dollars. Ah, Bixby . . ."

"Listen, I owe you thanks for the novel about my uncle. You gave me that pep talk about switching from stories to novels. The cash nexus, the novel as fungible artifact . . ."

"What a memory," Mettro said. "You'd be great in PR."

"Are you having fun?"

"It's a snap. I've got a job for you."

"Who said I wanted a job?"

"It's written all over you. You want to marry Manishin; a job can maybe make that happen. Listen, I was there when Bixby brought you into *The Communist Manifesto*—the new relations between people. *All that is solid melts into air.* . . . Don't forget I met Bixby before you. Did he ever tell you that Marx said the bourgeois genius was to make any human way of behaving morally okay— 'valuable' he called it, philosophically—as long as it becomes economically possible."

I laughed, nostalgically happy to be hearing the old rhetoric from when we were young, after the war.

"No," I said. "There were some conversations he'd had with the old boy which Bixby kept to himself. But I remember *you* preaching me the financial gospel of the novel versus the short story. Look around you," I said, a wave of my arm indicating the free grass, the free cottages, and, less visibly but all around us, nevertheless, the free time to sweat out my slow-in-coming third novel. "Pretty valuable. Free, in fact."

"Nothing's free," Mettro said. "Listen to this." He

closed his eyes and muttered, "I hope I can still remember. It's been a while. *The bourgeoisie has resolved all honor and dignity into*—Shit! I've lost it."

"Hold it," I said, willing and eager to continue the game. "I've got my copy of *The Manifesto* here." I returned from my cottage and tossed it at him. It was, of course, *not* my copy, but Bixby's tattered relic, which had helped to change my life, for wrong or right. It felt good to be the tosser of the book for once. He leafed the pages with dazzling speed and continued: "*. . . resolved all honor and dignity into exchange-value.*" More wild leafing. "*The bourgeoisie has transformed the doctor, the lawyer, the priest, the poet, the man of science into its paid wage-laborers.*"

"This means," I said, "that I should get a job?"

"Well—"

"You know," I said, "you and Bixby both, for years, every time you talk about Marx or quote Marx it's really about how extraordinary the bourgeoisie is. What kind of Marxism *is* this? If I should be transformed into a paid wage-laborer, in whose God-damned name is it? The old or the new?"

"No, no, no . . ." Mettro got excited. "Marx sees modern bourgeois culture as part of modern industry. You realize how long ago he saw that? My God! He was the fucking first! I'm talking about 1868."

"But he seems to—so approving . . ."

"No, it's just that he knows that whether you create pictures, books, or industrial products, it's all the marketplace. *In the meantime!* Until Socialism, Communism, or any version of the real ultimate thing! We're in the U.S. *That's the meantime.*"

"Ah," I said, "the great 'meantime.'" I threw my arms out into the yellow sunshine. "Mettro," I said. "That's why I'm here. California is just another word for 'meantime.'" I closed my eyes against the pastel haze. "Manishin and I came to a big, endless 'meantime.' And this offer came along."

Mettro leaned back and propped the beat-up paperback against his narrow chest, insulated by its gray vest. "What's Manishin's 'meantime'?"

"She doesn't want to support me and make me a child."

"In short—she wants you to enter the marketplace."

"A paid wage-laborer . . . or else stop pushing to get married? Maybe something like that. Actually she's amazingly pure—she's happy to keep things the way they are. Is that suit made of silk?"

"Right."

"It's nice."

"Are you forgetting what I told you about the short story and the novel?"

"Are you kidding? It's what got me this deal. The novel is the hard currency. I owe you."

Mettro sat up and tossed *The Communist Manifesto* back at me. I dropped it and it fell into a clump of dry leaves.

"Listen," he said. "I have a theory about you: you are a potential Public Relations Magnate." (For a moment I thought he'd said Magnet and thought he was joking or sun-struck.) "Don't laugh," he went on. "You attract people; they see you as some kind of symbol, or some kind of Human Resource Opportunity." Mettro was talking in capital letters now and growing impassioned.

"Like Bixby," he said, "and that teacher at school you told me about. And your gambler uncle. People want to get involved in you." I thought—like Bixby he's exhorting me. Mettro was right; something in me made people exhort me, made them want to take me in hand, to convince me of one or another course of action for my life. Mettro himself was doing it while describing it.

"And that's why you could be a public relations whiz. So it's not writing fiction, but it's fiction of another kind. Manipulating metaphors, painting images. You'd be a great success. People will believe you because they'll want to be involved with what you're becoming."

"That's not for me."

"It doesn't matter. You're for it! The job is in New York—the East Coast branch of Rogers & Cowan. You'll love it."

"But I just *got* here!"

"No rush. You can start in two weeks," Mettro said blithely. "I should have brought my bathing suit. I don't have any appointments until five o'clock." He smiled a California smile, white-toothed, delighting in innocent evil. "I told you it was an easy dollar. Meantime."

"I'll lend you a bathing suit," I said. "Enjoy yourself. But the answer is: No!"

Before I fell asleep that night I decided. There are exhortations and there are exhortations. Bixby the believer, Bixby the keeper of the Marxist/Modernist flame, the seller of fantasy in an unimaginative world: he had earned the right to change my life. His message made sense. And it had led me into a career which kept me broke but also kept me in touch with something of value in myself. Mettro's proposition was another matter. As if he'd heard me and wished to convince me otherwise, Mettro called the next day and invited me to go with him to a party. "I hear Bixby may show," he said.

Bixby showed. He looked not a day older. Tanned, tubercular-thin, and gay, he shone like a bright jagged piece of bottle glass in that crowd of smooth-edged agents, producers, screenwriters, and public relations magnets. He played the piano, unheard but rapt; played only music I'd never heard before. Not a note of Scriabin. What had happened to the great Scriabin revolution? I'd been afraid that when he saw me there would be some embarrassment over the money he owed me. But debts apparently shared a special amnesia with Scriabin. And, it turned out, with his former religion of Modernism and fantasy.

I made a stab at getting his attention, one attempt to revive his old love for the young disciple I'd once been.

"Did you know that Molotov's real name was Scriabin? It turns out he was actually a relative of the composer." I meant, of course, to point out how mysteriously History and Music had come together in the Bixby I remembered. The point hung, fresh, in the air until Bixby staled it with a remark.

"Are you still doing that kind of thing?" he said. "That's all dead and buried. Stalin buried *The Communist Manifesto* and the funeral is being held all over Eastern Europe. It's *sauve qui peut*, now."

The Bixby I'd known spoke no French. But if *he* could believe it was every man for himself, how well had I known him, my comic-book Master?

"The name of the game is Romanticism," Bixby said, looking about him, distracted.

"All that is solid melts into air . . ." I hazarded. "The bourgeois period . . ."

"No, no, for God's sake. It was always only what you could imagine. That's why I'm trying to get some assignments writing music for movies . . . for TV. Romantic music—that never dies. The best-kept secret in modern times is this equation: *Marxism is Modernism and Modernism is Romanticism."* He spoke, still, in italics and left me to digest this aperçu while he played William Walton's Violin Concerto on the stereo for a producer who undoubtedly did not know that Bixby could not read or write music. It didn't matter, because in a few moments Bixby was the center of the party, elegantly miming a waltz passage as a waltzing violinist, sans violin, but with a skeletal dancing grace. He drew applause, laughter, and the arm of a pretty model five inches taller. Later, when he had left with her, I heard someone behind me sketch out Bixby's present life in a few choice California sentences.

"It better be *her* place," the voice of Los Angeles said. "Because he's living with Paul Randolph. There's only one bed. When Paul has the rent money, Paul gets the bed and Bixby gets the floor; when Bixby has it, Bixby gets the bed. Bixby has yet to pay a month's rent." Outside in the Beverly Hills night, facing the long curved floodlit driveway, I had a replayed vision of Bixby—not my remembered or fantasized Bixby, but the flesh Bixby, pushed by the pump of blood flushing the bony red face, the physical presence of the man as he'd waltzed with his invisible violin to the Walton concerto (had he not played Scriabin in waltz time at the Arthur Murray Dance Studio in those G.I. Bill days of long ago?). The words were all different now, but Bixby was unchanged. I'd been taken in by words! Bixby had preached a particular kind of Communist sainthood, the Gospel According to Saint Marx, and then coolly danced on, apparently taking his anarchic life day by day. Leaving me (or so it felt at that end-of-the-evening moment) to dance the Bixby Waltz— and end up in disappointment and poverty.

Behind me, through the French doors, I caught a glimpse of Mettro looking for me. He was my ride home— but I did not want to see him. Better even the unthinkable thought of a bus in Southern California. The next morning I called Mettro and reversed my decision. I was sick of the way my private relations had worked out. I was ready to try Mettro's public relations.

Of course the day I arrived in New York, Manishin warned me she was not to be bought—or even rented— by my change in employment status. Lying entangled in that long red hair I said, "Let's get married."

"Let's be friends," she said.

"Let's do both."

"I'm not sure that can be done."

"Are you in love?"

"Yes."

"Am I in love?"

"Yes."

"Then we're in love . . ."

"You're just conjugating. Look, I've *been* married. If you want, forget Shaw, forget all the social stuff. Something mysterious, something peculiarly chemical, happens when people get married. They stop being themselves . . . they start to represent things; it's all a nutty masquerade. A balance of power without countries. Give me a toke, will you?"

"You smoke too much of that stuff." I took a deep draw myself and waited for illumination. Nothing! I handed it back and asked Manishin, "Has it ever occurred to you that there's something odd about our friends—the ones who have been swallowed up by California?"

"Odd?"

"They're hooked on Marxism."

"A lot of that going around."

"But it's a strange kind—all about the past and the present. I thought it was supposed to be about the future. What I get from our friends is the bourgeois this, the bourgeois that. Never a word about the working class or suffering proletarians. And they never talk about Russia, which is supposed to be the future. Mettro says it's because we're living in the 'meantime.' "

"Between what and what?"

"It's like they're giving lessons in How to Survive Until the Revolution Comes. But not a word about how great it will be afterwards. Strange."

Manishin yawned. "Nothing personal," she said.

"It's two A.M. I'm on California time but you're not."

"Mmmmm."

"Put it out and let's go to sleep."

"Hey, don't husband me."

"I've got an idea. You keep your name, how's that?"

"Thanks," she said dryly. "It was always mine. And we can both lose everything else."

"Can any two people be with each other as much or as closely any other way?"

Another yawn. "Shaw says marriage is the most licentious of institutions. It combines the maximum of temptation with the maximum of opportunity."

"How was his marriage?"

"Unconsummated, they say."

"Ah, Manishin, you lawyer. Stop tempting me part-time. Marry me!"

That summer, in the year 1955, I joined Rogers & Cowan as a junior account executive at seven thousand dollars a year. In 1956 Manishin and I were married. Mettro flew east to be the triumphant best man. By 1963 I was making seventy thousand dollars a year. The go-go sixties were on their way. Manishin's two daughters were happy with me; their father, after serving a brief term in jail for forging checks, vanished into the midwest, from which hiding place Manishin never attempted to extradite him.

But how to tell about those years. The Romantic poets were wrong—youth is not like a dream. Youth is sharp, clear, surreal, flooded by the sunny light of memory and hope. It's when your life seems to *begin*, when you seem to set your feet on a continuing path, that the years go by as in a dream. That's how it was with our life together.

Friends were made, groups came together, broke apart; children had accidents; once I contracted a strange fever and almost died, but recovered, still undiagnosed but alive. Manishin gained fifteen pounds, lost them again, and turned down an appointment as state supreme court judge; a long ribbon of trivia, dramatic and banal by turns.

But what was the point of those years? Just look at two high points. Two years after Mettro introduced me to the golden days and nights of public relations, he went private. Suddenly he was just—gone. Not a word to anyone. Certainly no one at the office could find out where he was. It took months for information to drift in. He was in France, it turned out, living with a Japanese dancer. The gray suits had, apparently, been turned in for Basque sport shirts, a beret, and a carved walking stick. One of Manishin's colleagues had seen him so attired at a café in a small village in Provence. That was the early information. The later information was even more interesting. It seemed that Mettro's venture into freedom from commerce had been financed by his being on the take. Several of Rogers & Cowan's best clients affirmed this. Ah, Mettro, Pied Piper of the rat race, who led me in only to flee, himself. No one was very surprised. Except me. I was, as usual in these matters, astonished.

The name of the village was Menerbes; so small, I was warned, it didn't have a drugstore. I changed planes in Paris and flew to Nice where I rented the tiniest of cars, a Fiat, and drove North towards Avignon. At a town called

Cavaillon I stopped for lunch. I asked the waiter about Menerbes.

"Any Americans in Menerbes? *Est-ce qu'il y a des Américains à Menerbes?*" I said carefully.

"Why do you stop in Menerbes?" the waiter said. "They'll only serve you melons from Cavaillon."

"Life is not all melons," I said.

Apparently he disagreed, because the conversation ended there. I drove on, pondering what Manishin had said when I told her I was going to find Mettro.

"We can't afford the plane ticket," she'd told me. "But I'm glad you're going."

"Why?"

"Because just once you're going to confront one of those voices you've listened to. You're going to ask it—"

"—about the Unity of Theory and Practice," I butted in.

"What's that?"

"It's a notion in philosophy. I forget where it started—but it ends up in Marx. And Mettro—with all his talk about the cash nexus—never once mentioned stealing or crime. He talked about the making of money as if it were the healthiest, most natural activity in the world. Not a hint of any fascination with the criminal, with the underground imagination. My Uncle Irving had a number going in that direction. But that was different. That was *my* inheritance, which I decided, a long time ago, to ignore except by writing about it."

"Do we *know* that Mettro stole the money for his great getaway? I'd hate for you to be embarrassed after flying thousands of miles."

"It was nothing so gross as simple stealing. Quite elegant, this woman at the L.A. office said. She called it 'skimming.' Apparently if you skim long enough, you end up with a great big pot of money—and because you didn't take it all at once it's hard to trace."

I couldn't articulate for Manishin, or yet for myself, the sense that I might have run into a Bixby/Mettro Marxism that was weird but, somehow, very American. A Marxism designed to make the middle class feel okay; to make the privileged comfortable in their skins, in their selfishness. A Marxism in which the working class is, as usual, invisible.

In a run-down café at the top of the village perched on a steep hill I found my man. There were almost as many dogs as there were patrons. Mettro was wearing a purple-and-orange sport shirt and a navy-blue beret. I decided on a light approach; no heavy-handed morality. The trick was to find out what had really happened and why. Mettro was going through a pile of photographs with great care. When I sat down across the table from him he looked up and smiled.

"Well," he said. "I was wondering if you'd be in touch one way or another." He handed me a batch of the photographs . "I've been discovering some new talents. Like photography. What do you think?"

They were carefully posed shots of a pretty young Japanese woman. Her face was flat, like the surface of a Matisse painting, the eyes staring mischievously at the camera, sometimes directly, sometimes over her shoulder, a parody of high-fashion magazine photographs.

"Terrific," I said. "Who's the model?"

"Ishekenawa. Here she comes."

And she appeared moving delicately from the dark interior of the café to the sunny table where we sat. She was startlingly tall for a Japanese woman, and she wore a simple loose robe.

"Ishekenawa." Mettro gestured towards me, and then burst into a babble (to me) of Japanese in the midst of which I heard my first and last names; obviously an introduction.

"She doesn't speak any English," Mettro said. "Have some red wine. Local stuff. That's what we drink here in the afternoons in Menerbes."

"Just coffee. I don't want to fall over."

The coffee was foul, the café shoddy; Mettro had not escaped to a jewel thief's exotic Riviera; but Ishekenawa was exquisitely made, with small shapely breasts and long, long legs, and the warm Provençal sun, a steady scent of lavender in the air, and the sloping hills down to the valley were thrilling. So Mettro had bought a mixed bag of Paradise with his subtle "skimming." I was shaky with jet lag and it was not the time to evaluate anything. It was the time to ask what I'd come to ask. (I'm not sure I could have done it if Ishekenawa spoke English.)

"Is it true?"

He didn't play games, for which I gave him instant credit. No "Is *what* true?" and the usual sparring.

"Of course," Mettro said. "The idea of taking the money

occurred to me a few times and I blocked it out as wrong
or dangerous or both. Then one day I was daydreaming
after a client lunch—General Electric, big stuff, they
wanted us to help them diversify, maybe get into show
business, and I was trying to get revved up to work on the
account even though I was full of Chateaubriand and
brandy—I was actually more fed up with the work than I
admitted to myself—and I suddenly remembered a passage from, oh, I forget, it's either *Das Kapital* or *The
Communist Manifesto* or *Theses on Feuerbach*—something explaining why capitalism would have to fall—this
memory, by the way, was like a dream—anyway the idea
was that because the giant corporations would finally have
to merge and become international monopolies and car-
tels, like GE for example (those are the new words, after
it happened, that's not what Marx called them) . . ."

"Are you sure you're telling me what happened or the
rationale for what you did ?"

"It's the same thing," Mettro said. Ishekenawa watched
both of us, intently. "So," Mettro continued, "squeezed
by the laws affecting international expansion and the
demands of bigger and bigger trade unions, the corporations would be ripe for overthrow by the workers. But
then," Mettro took off his beret and wiped his forehead
of the midday Provençal sweat, "then there was a mention of something I'd never thought of. Marx says: *Of
course the possibilities of bribery and other illegal means
of prolonging the life of the free marketplace are endless.*
That was a big moment."

"A big moment for *you?*"

"A flash of light in the darkness of Southern California. I mean the same as you and all of us normal middle-class characters trying to get ahead and make sense of life at the same time, I always assumed that things like Bribery or Theft, criminal activities with capital letters in the front of the words, were done by Others."

"I used to steal books," I said.

"And I stole money from my father's pants," Mettro said. "Youthful high jinks. A kind of complaint through action."

I was getting a clear picture, for the first time, why Mettro was good at public relations. He had a phrase for everything. All you needed was the right phrase. The trick was: never be at a loss. Which meant: never be at a loss for words.

"But if bribery could actually hold off socialism, extend the criminal life of capitalism—then why not seize the day. *Carpe diem.* The really bad stuff—bribing people, real stealing—was a little like murdering somebody. Or, at least, it was clearly criminal. It had nothing to do with the middle class—with people like us. But suddenly, I saw it differently. I saw myself bribing one of the people at GE to work out some 'skimming' of fees to the agency. And here's the key—*suddenly I saw it as simply taking on a partner and starting a new business venture.*"

"Listen," I said. "I changed my mind. I'll have some of that wine."

Mettro called out, *"S'il vous plaît,"* and got me a glass of the local red.

I drank up and leaned towards him trying to ignore Ishekenawa's steady, quiet presence and gaze. This was the moment I'd come for. (Actually that moment was to arrive a little after midnight, but I couldn't know that, yet.)

"Listen," I said, intensely, "you know, now, that was all just game-playing, just word magic, right? You know exactly what you did and that all this partner bullshit was just so you could get yourself to be a crook. It has nothing to do with any of the stuff you fed me about the cash nexus and fungible artifacts and, how does it go, the bourgeoisie has resolved all honor and dignity into exchange value . . . something like that . . ."

Mettro grinned happily at me: a teacher proud of his student. "No," he said, "not something like that. That's *exactly* how it goes."

"You know, I feel involved in this stuff—what you've done."

"I know. You're wrong, but I understand."

"I mean it's like you and I were partners before and now you've taken in new partners with a very different idea. A scary idea."

"That's why you came all this way, right? To understand. I assume you're not going to turn me in. You could have done that in New York."

"You assume, as usual, correctly."

"Where are you staying?"

"I didn't make reservations. I was told this town didn't even have a drugstore, but I figured there'd be some kind of hotel or pension."

"Never mind. You'll stay with us."

He blew off some more Japanese steam at Isheke-nawa. She nodded and kept her gaze on me.

"Absolutely not! No way!" I said.

•

Mettro's house was a simple one on the top of a steep street. Three stories but small—stone and wood, reddish. The real news was out in back. Three cars: a red Jaguar convertible, a BMW, and a Maserati. The Maserati's hood was up; it was more of a Mettro work-in-progress than a finished car. I think I was looking at seventy-five thousand dollars' worth of automotive equipment.

"A ride?" Mettro said.

I shook my head. A ride would implicate me even more. I had come to ask questions, to judge, to understand. I was not going to become the newest partner.

We whirled up and down those narrow streets, the three of us crammed into the silly seat; I was laughing against my will, Mettro twirling the wheel, Ishekenawa not laughing but smiling a broad distant smile. Later, over dinner at a small outdoor restaurant, just six tables in a sort of garden, a place of dreamy charm called Chez Marie, Mettro ordered more of the local wine and I drank too much of it.

"Do you know," I said to Mettro in mournful reproach, "because of you I'm a published novelist? Was."

"I know," Mettro said.

"Do you know," I continued, "that because of you I'm married to Manishin?"

"I know."

"But do you know that I don't know what I know?"

"I know. I've given up knowing what I know. The trick is—"

I stood up as swiftly as I could, given the wine and jet fatigue. But the point is: I stood up *before he could tell me, yet again, what the trick was.* I'd given up listening to Mettro.

Outside, a dry, lavender breeze struck me in the face and across the knees. Mettro and Ishekenawa got me into the car, then into the house, then, with a little more of a struggle, upstairs and into a bed.

I woke into the unaccustomed stitch of night-insect sounds and lavender smells with a desperate urge to pee. When I left the bathroom, I found Ishekenawa standing outside. Stupid with sleep and the early start of a hangover, but ever the *bourgeois gentilhomme,* I gestured towards the bathroom door and said, "Do you have to—" She took my arm and guided me back towards my bedroom.

"Are you feeling better?" she asked. "I couldn't sleep."

"I thought you couldn't speak English."

She stretched out next to me and reached up the longest arm I'd ever seen and snapped off the bedside lamp. The moon kept pouring in through the open shutters, so much moonlight that the lamp being off made no difference. Ishekenawa kissed me.

"What is this?" I said. And then, suspicious again, "Did *he* send you in?"

"He's asleep."

Her skin smelled like lavender soap and she answered questions like Mettro, without answering anything. He could have sent her in *and* been asleep, by now. Who knows what he might have in mind? Perhaps buying me off; Ishekenawa, another one of his famous fungible artifacts; adding pimping to skimming now that he had joined my Uncle Irving on the other side of the law. *Carpe diem*, my ass, I thought as I started to explore Ishekenawa. If I wasn't involved before, I am now.

It wasn't until the morning, when I woke, alone and starving, that it occurred to me that she might have simply been attracted to me and been moved, on her own, to betray Mettro. I rejected the explanation and flew back to New York, from Nice, that afternoon, with Bixby and Mettro both behind me, at last.

At the duty-free shop in Paris, while waiting for the plane to New York to arrive at the gate, I bought bottles and bottles of perfume for Manishin. Chanel No. 5, Shalimar, White Shoulders—by the ounce, no micro-ounces and no eau de toilette, the real stuff. I knew I was overdoing it, inviting not responsive passion or gratitude but more likely a knowing irony from my knowing, ironic little redhead. I couldn't help myself.

Bixby had folded on me.

Mettro had run out.

Manishin was my last chance.

Which brings us to the other high point: the day Manishin decided to leave me. The reasons were both elusive and somehow beside the point. The sandpaper of ordinary married life had rubbed off the sensitive skin of money, sex, power, helplessness. All the things everybody ends up fighting about—no matter how special they think they are.

Here is Manishin after I have given her several pieces

of luggage she had forgotten in the bedroom closet. She is sipping her drink and, with my encouragement, is expatiating on one small but central point I'd missed: why she had to leave.

"Don't go," I said.

"I warned you."

"That was years ago."

"Makes no difference. True is true."

"But I love you, you love me, I loved you, you loved me."

"You're still conjugating. Changing tenses doesn't change anything. I told you—we were better off as friends. Everybody is. I warned you people stop being themselves when they get married. You can't be friends if you're not yourself." As always Manishin was in the advance guard. Half the people we knew were choosing to live together, or apart, as "friends" instead of getting married. *Time* magazine did cover stories; *The New Yorker* did a profile. Years later, marriage would again regain its status as the privileged class in the class structure of relationships. But for now, as usual, Manishin was ahead of her time. Old George Bernard Shaw would have been proud of her.

"Okay," I said desperate, adaptive, "let's be friends. We'll live together."

Manishin flashed a smile. "You're missing the point, again. You always have."

"What do you mean?"

She sighed. It was to be an unusual moment. Sighs were not in the Manishin repertoire. "The point you missed," she said very slowly, "is simply that love, ambition, literary and financial, Modernism, Marxism—all that stuff, they're just a chorus of voices singing at you all your life, since you were a kid. There was always somebody to tell you what you should do or think or feel. And you got caught up in the web of words. It's words that made you miss the point. You listened—oh, God, you're a great listener. But what you never did was . . . look . . . to see what the people you believed actually did. Bixby turned you onto *la vie bohème*—then quietly went Hollywood Anarchist Romantic. Mettro sucked you into the rat race and then hit out for the expatriate life in France on funny money. But there must have been something to tip you off that they weren't what they seemed. You're a real artist—an artist at Missing the Point! And even with us, just now, you—"

"Missed—"

"Right!"

I took a deep breath and then took a chance. "Was it—Ishekenawa?"

"No."

"I told you it never happened before and never happened again. It was like being run over. An accident!"

"Who ran over who?"

"It *was* Ishekenawa!"

"It was you. I just can't go on being married to Candide." She jumped up and paced around me. "THIS IS MY LIFE, DAMMIT, NOT THE BLUEBIRD OF HAPPINESS." As usual, I missed the references. I had read neither Voltaire nor Maeterlinck. "Even," she continued, whirling around me like a prosecuting imp in an imaginary court, "Even if you and I agreed on whether or not you participated in an act of white slavery . . ."

"White slavery?"

"You said you knew what Mettro was up to."

"I said I *thought* he *might* have been up to something . . ."

She sat down, suddenly exhausted of all that frenetic energy.

"Anyway—she wasn't the point. If you would promise to stop listening, stop thinking, stop developing worldviews, stop latching onto ideas about life and how it should be lived . . ."

"I will . . . *I will!*"

"No," Manishin said. "You'll promise. And, worse, you might even do it. Then I'd hate you. Because the real horror is—that Candide stuff I hate about you is also what pulled me to you. It's hopeless."

Now it was my turn to be drained of energy; of hope, actually.

"You mean you think I'll always—"

"Miss—"

"The . . ."

"Point." Manishin popped the word at me, like a period in a life sentence. "The only way for us to be friends, now, is to break up. We've done the other thing. So, here I go." She hefted her luggage and kissed me on the mouth, cool and dry. She is gone now; I am on my own.

Again, or at last.

Bixby, Mettro, Manishin—you've met them. But what of Marx?

Myself: Maurice Marx, my grandfather a second cousin,

once removed, to Karl Marx. Thus, I am a direct descendant of Karl: a second cousin, thrice removed. And if
you've wondered why I had never read any of the stuff
Bixby, Mettro, and Manishin were laying on me, just think
about my father growing up in a Viennese bourgeois home
with a mother full of family pride about her connection
to the scourge of middle-class Europe. Thus, our entire
side of the family removed themselves from any connection to the life of thought. Thought carried a bomb in its
hand and a knife in its teeth, promising new worlds and
destroying old ones. My father, the son of a medieval
scholar, became the first Marx on his side of the family
to skip college and go right into business. The rest of us,
too, avoided education as the first step towards communist damnation.

And I, a refugee child, as nervous about my name as I
might have been had it been the middle of World War
One, when people with German names were being ostracized or turned in to the FBI, only I knew that I was not
an innocent Marx—but a real one. A relative of HIM
SELF. The Ur-Marx. Now, having thought much about
this, and having, finally, read all I could of and about
him, I think I rather take after him.

I admire the old man immensely. Only those who
plunge headlong towards a point end up missing it so
completely. Marx, by jumping ferociously at an economic, materialist view of the universe, missed the point
of the psychological—that monkey wrench in the
machinery of theory. And I, heir to old Karl, continued
in the family tradition.

I was ready for any explanation—any guide to the jungle of reality. As long as it had nothing to do with the subtle confusions of personality, the ambiguity of motives, the fact that my Uncle Irving might have been not an existential hero of the delicately criminal gesture but— simply a psychopath nut who was out to lose, to get caught, and to finally simply enjoy the pleasure of weaving a web of philosophical explanation around a compulsion; that Bixby might have been only a garbage can of failed received ideas; the very rancidness of whose mixture— Dianetics, Marx turned upside down to become Joyce and T. S. Eliot—was what attracted me to him—just a *Luft-mensch* hustling exhortations in return for loans divisible by eighteen—his only hold on Life . . . that Mettro might have been not a poet of self-interest, a singer in the entr'acte between the past opera of selfish capitalism and the future opera of altruistic socialism—his precious "meantime"—in whose lyrics I'd heard another of my songs of salvation . . . but simply a California con man en route to his ultimate destiny, like many a con man, surviving on the lam through silence, exile, and cunning.

Thinking about this now, surrounded by the luggage-debris of a marriage, I wonder if the essential trouble comes, perhaps, from the fact that we do not live alone; that we live in the world. There are other voices out there from the start. How to know when to listen and when to be oblivious? How to know which point is *the* point? It's difficult. The inner voice is soft, tentative. It often seems to be without any point at all. The temptation to listen to others is very great. As soon as they speak—*all that is solid melts into air. . . .*

That is the general condition. But there is also the specific. My father, brother, and I came to this country as refugees from Austria in 1940. My brother deaf from a childhood accident, my father a dispossessed businessman, merely deaf to other people's ideas; willful and stubborn. It fell to me to pick up all the hints, nuances, directions that could help us find our way in a strange place. Foreigners must listen to what the natives tell them. In such ways are lifetime habits formed. My brother is now a surgeon in Tulsa, Oklahoma, with his hearing restored by several operations. My father lives, retired, in Florida, where he has grown more malleable with age. He is now, however, quite deaf. And I—I have just listened to Manishin say goodbye.

Even at this point, a grown man, I am ready to listen to others. Finally, too, it is a matter of faith. There is no other way to take or refuse the world, except on faith. It's too hard to prove anything. I won't even bother to play around with the now commonplace notion that the Marxist idea is and was a question of belief, replacement for old, dead religions, et cetera, et cetera. That's just another opinion and I'm through with the scrimmage of opinion.

I'm interested in knowing or *not* knowing. Was Bixby's grandmother really Welsh and his grandfather really Indian? Which one was Jewish? Is Scriabin really a great and neglected composer—or the second-rate mystic maker

of program music he's often thought to be? Did Manishin really want her independence—or did she want me
to overwhelm her with reasons to get married? How deaf
is my father? Sometimes he seems to hear quite well,
other times—such as when I try to explain to him about
Manishin and our breaking up—total, reproachful silence.

I am pouring myself another vodka from the bottle with
the tall spear of buffalo grass floating mysteriously in its
depths. I stare at it closely. It looks like any other tall
blade of grass. How does it impart that odd, yellowish
color to the vodka and that special slightly briny flavor to
the usually colorless, tasteless liquid? I'm sure a scientist
could tell me. But, in spite of what Manishin says, looking may be as complicated a route to knowledge as listening.

Still, I can't complain. My mistakes have all given me
something. My work in public relations is as easy and
lucrative as the otherwise dishonest Mettro promised. The
clients often ask to have "the writer" assigned to their
accounts, knowing that I once published short stories and
novels, too difficult to read, but elegant to refer to. It gives
a different kind of satisfaction than Bixby and I had in
mind for my career. But a satisfaction, nevertheless. Other
satisfactions impend, too. A young woman at the office,
hair not so red as Manishin's, mind not so sharp, but
still . . .

I will finish the bottle and go to sleep. I will sleep a
slightly murky sleep; sleep the color of yellowish buffalo-
grass vodka; sleep secured by the sense of resting in a
universe of "missed points": religion, art, war (its G.I.
Bills and its Bixbys), commerce, economics (and its Met-

tros), philosophy, love (and its Manishins). I was afraid to sleep alone this first night. But now I know I am not alone. If it is, finally, in the nature of all points that they be missed, then everyone in the world may sleep safely in that sweet security.

The party in my head is over. Good night Bixby, good night Mettro, good night Manishin, good night.

DATE DUE

Demco, Inc. 38-293